And Through the Trembling Air

Michael C. Keith

BLUE MUSTANG

P R E S S

Blue Mustang Press
Boston, Massachusetts

First printing

ISBN 978-1-935199-10-6
PUBLISHED BY BLUE MUSTANG PRESS
www.BlueMustangPress.com
Boston, Massachusetts

Printed in the United States of America

Acknowledgments

The stories contained in this volume first appeared in *Grey Sparrow Journal, Lowestoft Chronicle, The Absent Willow Review, Danse Macabre, Cynic Magazine, Einstein's Pocket Watch, The Fabulist, Aurora Wolf, Melusine, Whiskey Creek Press, Outward Ink, Sleet Magazine,* and *Cantaraville Quarterly.*

Very special appreciation is owed Susanne Riette-Keith, Chris Sterling, and Nicki Sahlin for their invaluable comments and suggestions. All the stories are better for their astute and generous input.

The author may be reached via his website: www.michaelckeith.com

Also by Michael C. Keith

Contents

Through all the changing scenes of life.
—Nahum Tate

The Waiting Bell

Your children innocent and charming as the beasts
— W.H. Auden

"*Nein!*" protested Hadelin Guttmeyer, sobbing as the village doctor, Ruland Bruhier, declared her nine-year-old daughter, Elfi, dead. "*Nein!* Look at her. The blush is yet in her cheeks."

"I am so sorry, *Frau* Guttmeyer, but her heart has ceased to beat. She has no pulse," replied the doctor, sympathetically.

"But why?" asked Ludwig Guttmeyer, clutching his wife. "Elfi was not ill until days ago and then only weak? Why so sudden? Surely God would not do this to us."

"I cannot explain her illness. Something drew her strength away. There are many things that defy medical understanding, even in these modern times," answered the doctor, abashedly. "But, alas, dead is dead…regrettably."

"You said that about others during the plague and many were buried alive," snapped Hadelin, caressing the forehead of her daughter.

"That is nonsense! How do you know of such things thirty years later? Rumors. All foolish gossip," countered Dr. Bruhier indignantly while closing his medical bag. "I'll have the undertaker come for the body."

9

"She is not even cold. Life is still in her. *Nein*, we will take her to the Waiting House in Freiburg," answered Mrs. Guttmeyer, looking at her husband for support.

"Look!" blurted Ludwig Guttmeyer, pointing at his daughter's twitching hand. "You see *Herr* Doctor, Elfi is with us still."

"That is a post mortem muscle spasm," observed the doctor coolly, as he donned his overcoat. "Believe as you wish, and do as you must. Whatever gives you peace, but I tell you she is gone. Good day, *Herr* Guttmeyer... *Frau* Guttmeyer."

As the doctor departed, the Guttmeyers lifted their daughter's inert body in their arms and softly wept as they plied her pale face with kisses.

"Ludwig, feel. She is warm. She is not with God yet," uttered his wife.

"In the morning we will take her to Beckenhauer's," responded Mr. Guttmeyer gravely.

"Yes... yes, and she will return to us," added Hadelin Guttmeyer, pressing her daughter's limp hand against her father's tortured face.

That night Elfi's parents maintained a prayer vigil beside their daughter's bed as she lay in repose, and at the first sign of dawn, they carried her to the dining room table where her mother prepared her for the ride to Beckenhauer's Waiting House. As Mr. Guttmeyer readied the carriage, his wife dressed Elfi in her favorite frock. Images of her daughter waltzing merrily about the cottage in the new pink and white dress she'd received for her birthday just weeks earlier made her chest heave in sorrow. Yet the belief that her daughter might still be alive kept her from complete collapse.

"*Mein liebling*, come back. We love you so," whispered Hadelin into her daughter's ear, and in that instant she was convinced Elfi's eyelid moved. "*Liebste*, we wait for you with all our heart."

In the dim morning light, Mr. Guttmeyer placed his beloved child in the back of the carriage. Wrapped in a thick family quilt, her small face was barely visible as the family horse began to move down the dirt road leading from their cottage to their somber destination. Along the way, neither Guttmeyer uttered a word, lost as they were in their own precious memories of their only offspring.

The November wind created vortexes of the dried leaves that lay in deep layers along the winding road to the Beckenhauer's Waiting House, and by the time the Guttmeyers reached it, their modest carriage looked as if it had been deliberately adorned for the Autumn Fest that coincidentally was in progress in nearby Freiburg.

"What has happened to the Waiting House?" inquired Hadelin to her husband as he tightened the reigns on his horse to bring them to a stop. "Oh, Ludwig, what is going on?"

It appeared that the once formidable structure was being dismantled. The elder Mr. Beckhenhauer approached them from the pile of recently removed lumber beside the Waiting House, tossing his ax to the ground.

"*Guten tag*! May I help you?" he said as the Guttmeyers climbed from their carriage.

"We bring our sleeping daughter to your Waiting House, *Herr* Beckenhauer," they answered in unison.

"It is no longer operating. You can see it is being torn down to make way for a dairy barn," replied the senior Beckenhauer.

"But why? Our daughter is not dead, though the doctor says she is. We wish her to wait here until she comes back to us," said Hadelin Guttmeyer, clutching her fists to her breasts.

"*Es tut mir leid.* It is too late. There have been no patrons in three years, so we must find another means of income. Once the waiting house was full, but now people do not seem worried about burying their loved ones before they are truly dead. Now we must get by on Mrs. Beckenhauer's birthing work."

"Please take in our daughter. We will pay what you ask. It will not take long for she will return soon. *Ja*, Ludwig?"

"*Jawohl*, Elfi will soon be with us. Please let her rest here until she does, *Herr* Beckenhauer," pleaded Mr. Guttmeyer, reaching for the old man's hand. "The law will not allow us to keep her at home. As you know, when the doctor declares someone dead, they must be buried within two days."

"I am certainly familiar with that ordinance," replied Beckenhauer. "In fact, if a corpse is thought to be infectious, it must be disposed of immediately. Your daughter was not contagious, I presume?"

"Of course, not," answered Hadelin, indignantly. "Look for yourself. She does not appear to be dead, and there was no known cause for her affliction."

Mr. Beckenhauer lifted the blanket from Elfi's body and moved his face close to the little girl's.

"Children do not putrefy as quickly as the old. They may look asleep when, in fact, they are quite dead. She has no air from her mouth and no pulse," said the old man holding Elfi's wrist. "So she is more than likely in the Lord's care."

"Look at her face, *Herr* Backenhauer. It is as it was just days ago when she peeled the apples for the strudel I made. It was her favorite goody. She was so happy."

"But I have begun to destroy the waiting house, as you can see," protested Mr. Beckenhauer.

A small girl about Elfi's age approached and clutched Mr. Beckenbauer's hand.

"*Opa*, who is there?" she asked, standing on her toes to catch a glimpse inside the carriage.

"Please go back inside, Guita. I will be there shortly," said her grandfather tenderly.

"It's a little girl like me, *opa*," noted the child with curiosity.

"Yes, it is, sweetheart. Now go to your *oma*," replied Mr. Backenhauer, giving her a little push toward the house.

"Is she asleep, *opa*?"

"Yes, she is asleep," answered Mrs. Guttmeyer, smiling sweetly at the little girl.

"Can we play together when she wakes up?"

"But, of course, you may play with my Elfi when she awakes."

"Please, go to the house now, Guita," said Beckenhauer more firmly this time, and his granddaughter reluctantly obeyed.

After a pause, he returned his gaze to the small body in the carriage.

"Very well. We will take her for the week. That is all that is necessary to determine beyond any doubt her status," said Beckenhauer, resignedly.

"Bless you, sir," responded Hadelin Guttmeyer, her hands clasped as if in prayer.

"Take her to what is left of the waiting house," directed Beckenhauer. "If she comes back, I will notify you immediately, but you should not expect such a call."

"*Jawohl, Herr* Beckenhauer. We will await your call about our little Elfi," said Mr. Guttmeyer, taking the reins of his horse and moving the carriage to the building where his daughter would be stored.

After placing her still body on one of a row of tables inside the waiting house, the Guttmeyers kneeled beside her and prayed. They then reluctantly left her for their trip home.

"*Auf Wiedersehen*, my sweetheart," said Hadelin, waving to her daughter. "We will see you soon."

That afternoon, as the Guttmeyers returned north to their small farm, Beckenhauer restored several of the wood planks he'd removed from the waiting house to make certain Elfi's body would be shielded from the many wolves roaming the surrounding woods. Once, long ago, they had gained access to the waiting house and fed on four bodies in repose there. It had been a horrible experience for

Beckenhauer as relatives of the mauled demanded monetary compensation for their trauma, almost ruining him. He had carefully reinforced the building to prevent it ever happening again.

"It is like a fortress," his wife had observed.

"Exactly. Only God should take the flesh from those inside," Beckenhauer had replied, stoically.

It was nightfall when he was satisfied that the building would protect its contents. The only thing remaining to do was connect the young Guttmeyer to the waiting bell. It seemed a fruitless task to Beckenhauer, but he had promised the child's parents he would provide the services of his waiting house and he would not do otherwise.

When he entered the building, he was surprised to see his grandchild standing beside the table on which the Guttmeyer child rested.

"Guita, what are you doing here? This is not a place for you. Please return to the house. It is late and it will soon be time for supper."

"But *opa*, I heard her call my name," replied the girl.

"Nonsense. She cannot call your name. She doesn't know you. She cannot talk. Now I must connect her to the bell," said Beckenhauer, removing a spool of string from beneath the table.

"What are you doing, *opa*?"

"Tying her finger to the bell in case she comes back," replied the old man wrapping the end of the string to the bell that dangled a few feet above Elfi.

A thin wire ran from the bell to the house and connected to another bell that would also ring should the occupant show life.

"Come back, *opa*? But she is here," said Guita.

"*Nein*, my Guita. She is not here. Now go to the house."

"Let me tie the string to her finger. Please, may I?" pleaded Guita, in the way that melted her grandfather's resolve.

"Yes, okay, and then you must go. Here, now, place it around her forefinger and make a tight connection."

"But not too tight, *opa*. It will hurt her," rejoined Guita, looping the string into a bow.

"That will do. Thank you, Guita. You helped your *opa*. Now go to the house and tell *oma* I am on my way.

"Yes, *opa*," said Guita, as she scampered from the building.

That will not do, thought Beckenhauer, as he untied the bow replacing it with a strong knot on Elfi Guttmeyer's thin finger.

"*Gute nacht,* little one," muttered Beckenhauer as he doused the candle and went for his supper.

This particular November had been milder although far windier than usual, and on Elfi's first night ever away from home, hard gusts pounded the Beckenhauer compound, which included their cottage, two storage sheds, a privy, and the waiting house. Yet it wasn't the powerful blasts of air that suddenly awakened Guita. She was drawn from her dreams by the faint sound of a bell, or what she thought was one. In her dark bedroom she strained to detect another toll and was rewarded as a series of jingles rode the surging Autumnal tempest through the shuttered window to her ears. The chimes were accompanied by the barely discernable words of a child.

"Giuta, come. Let's play," beckoned a faint voice, and Guita slipped from her bed and made her way out of the house in the direction of the sounds, which led her to the waiting house.

With no sense of foreboding or fear, she entered the building and was greeted by Elfi, who stood atop her sleep table smiling. Until the stars faded and the eastern horizon brightened, they frolicked about the forest, dancing, singing, and playing. Guita had never felt such joy or fulfillment. After the loneliest year of her life, following the accidental drowning of her parents in the river, she now had a companion her own age and she felt great happiness.

Just before dawn, she slipped back into her grandparents' house

15

and returned to bed, quickly falling into such a deep sleep that her grandmother had to call her several times in order to awaken her an hour later.

"Sweetheart, you are so sleepy. It is time for breakfast," cajoled Mistress Beckenhauer.

"Oh, *oma*, I have the most wonderful friend," said Guita, rubbing the sleep from her heavy eyes.

"Who did you dream of?" inquired the old woman to her granddaughter.

"No, not a dream. A real friend," replied Guita, climbing out of bed and into her slippers.

"Now, who could that possibly be, child?"

"The little girl in the waiting house…Elfi. We played in the forest," answered Guita.

Mistress Beckenhauer's eyes widened and she took a step back from her grandchild, alarmed by her strange statement.

"What do you speak of, Guita? You had a dream," responded the woman, who then noticed several dried leaves clinging to her granddaughter's dressing gown. "How did you get these on you? You were outside?"

"Yes, *oma*, outside with Elfi…in the forest. It was such fun. Did you not hear the bell? She was calling my name."

"A dream, *mein liebling*…only a dream. Now come for your breakfast," said Mistress Beckenhauer, gathering the dead leaves from around Guita's feet.

"Good morning, Guita. You are very sleepy today…*ja*?" said Beckenhauer with his nose in his plate of sausages.

"Good morning, *opa*," replied Guita, kissing his cheek.

"Ah, cold lips need a hot breakfast. Sit *liebling* and eat your *wurste* before it cools."

Normally Guita could not get enough of her grandmother's special sausage, but this morning she felt oddly repulsed by the sight of it on her plate. Noticing her lack of enthusiasm, Mrs. Beckenhauer took one of the two sausages on Guita's plate and plopped it on her husband's.

"Sometimes young girls must watch their figures, Ludwig. Isn't that right, Guita?" winked Mrs. Beckenhauer to her granddaughter.

"Oh, I see. So you have a suitor? Well, he better not be over ten years old or I'll take the horse whip to him," joked Mr. Beckenhauer.

"*Opa*, I have a new friend," said Guita suddenly energized.

"A new friend?"

"Yes, I told *oma,* but she thinks I had a dream."

"And who is this new friend? A wood nymph?"

"It's Elfi…in the waiting house. She called to me with the bell last night. Did you not hear it either, *opa*?"

After a long silence, Mrs. Beckenhauer chimed in.

"She has an imagination like her poor dear mother had. Anja was always telling stories about imaginary friends and how they would play."

"But we did play, *oma* and *opa.* We chased the animals in the forest and climbed high in the trees to find the bird nests," protested Guita.

"Well, it is a good thing you did not fall from the treetops and bruise that pretty face of yours," replied Beckenhauer, shrugging his shoulders to his wife. "But I do not want you in the waiting house while that poor girl awaits burial."

"But *opa*, she is alive…"

"Please, let's not have any more of that nonsense. Now help *oma* clear the table. You will go into town with her today for supplies, and I think something special," said Beckenhauer, winking at his wife.

"Yes, *mein liebling,* we will purchase you a new jumper for the church dinner on Saturday. Come now," said Mrs. Beckenhauer, removing Guita's untouched plate.

"Like Elfi's with pink border?" asked Guita, brightening.

That evening, Guita went to bed early complaining of an upset stomach after barely touching one of her grandmother's special dishes. Besides dessert, there were few things that Guita loved more than *Leipziger Allerlei,* a thick soup made from a combination of vegetables and potato cubes and beef chunks.

"Poor child. Some hot chamomile tea and sleep and you will be your old self," assured her grandmother escorting her grandchild to her room.

Guita was exhausted and fell into a deep sleep almost instantly. When she awoke, the sun was peeking through the wood shutters.

"Hello, dear grandchild," greeted Mrs. Beckenhauer. "Breakfast is on the table. Come join grandpapa."

When she removed the quilt from Guita, she was startled to find dried mud on the girl's legs and sleeping gown.

"How did this get on you? Did you roam outside during the night?"

"No, *oma*…I don't think so", answered Guita, puzzled by the dirt clinging to her. "I did not wake up once, and I am still tired."

"Perhaps you went outside instead of using the chamber pot. That is what you did and don't remember. Here let me wash your feet and we'll have a good breakfast. *Opa* is waiting," said Mrs. Beckenhauer, pouring water from a vase onto a corner of her apron and wiping the stains from Guita's ankles.

"May I sleep a little longer, *oma*?" asked Guita leaning on her elbows.

"Certainly not. You had a long rest. There are things to do. We must add lace to the hem of your new dress for the Church dinner. Come, *mein liebling*," responded Mrs. Beckenhauer, leading Guita by the hand from her room.

"My princess, good morning," greeted Mr. Beckenhauer. "No more strange dreams, I hope?"

"No *opa,* I had no dreams at all," answered Guita, taking her place at the table.

As on the previous day, the sight of food did not have the usual positive effect on her. In fact, she could feel her stomach tighten at the sight of the steaming victuals.

"*Mutter*, can you imagine the rat traps were empty? Not a single carcass anywhere. Not even in the waiting house. They all had cheese. Nothing was nibbled on. It is the first time since the plague that has happened. Then, all the rats were killed to end the sickness. But they soon came back and have always taken the bait. Very odd, don't you think? The cats are nowhere to be found either. But I'm sure they all will...the rats, too," reported the elder Beckenhauer, chomping his sausage.

"Is Elfi still sleeping, *opa*?" asked Guita.

"*Ja,* my love. I'm afraid so. She will stay asleep. Friday her parents will take her home for burial."

"But *opa*, I do not think she will stay sleeping," replied Guita.

"I wish otherwise, too. She was a beautiful child, but she has lost the glow in her young flesh and her lips have thinned as they do in the dead...but do not fret, *liebling*. She will be one of God's favorite and be with the angels in Heaven. Now eat your breakfast before it is cold."

"I am not hungry, *opa*," said Guita, and her grandmother removed her dish.

"Very well. We cannot make you eat. You must still have the stomachache. Some more hot tea will give you strength. Now go take the dirty sheets from your bed, and I will bring you clean ones."

"Yes, *oma,*" answered Guita.

When Mrs. Beckenhauer brought the fresh linen to her granddaughter's bedroom, she found the girl fast asleep atop the soiled sheets. Later in the day, Guita had revived enough to help her grandmother trim her new frock. For the first time in two days, she began to feel her appetite return, and she pleased her grandparents by emptying most of her plate of goulash.

"It is good to see your appetite back, but you probably have no room for *oma's* cake," joked Mr. Beckenhauer.

"But I do, *opa*," protested Guita.

"Very well then, a large piece of *marmorkuchen* for you," announced Mrs. Beckenhauer, placing a wedge of the chocolate and marble cake before Guita, who suddenly felt nauseous and vomited her undigested goulash onto the table.

"Oh, *liebchen!*" cried Mr. Beckenhauer, leaping beyond the range of her eruption. "Look, *mutter*, I think some blood...*yes?*"

"Perhaps, papa. We will get the doctor if she does not improve," replied Mrs. Beckenhauer, taking hold of Guita's arm and leading her from the room.

She bathed her granddaughter and put her to bed, concluding her stomach malady had worsened.

"Sleep, young one. In the morning you will be well," said Mrs. Beckenhauer reassuringly. "Children soon recover from what ails them."

"Yes, *oma,* I will be well in the morning," said Guita, who soon slept deeply.

The wind blew with even greater intensity than it had in recent days and the shutters on Guita's room rattled loudly, but it was not the wind that awakened her in the middle of the night. It was the ringing of the bell in the waiting house, accompanied again by Elfi's voice beckoning her.

"Come, Guita. Let us play," urged her nocturnal companion, and Guita rose and slipped from the house recalling she had done exactly the same thing the night before when they had chased the grey wolves from their den across the moonlit forest and merrily spun with the leafy whirligigs across frost covered fields.

For the next two nights, Guita joined Elfi as their playing turned to hunting, and they tracked and slew rabbits, red squirrels, and hedgehogs. Guita had never felt such joy and could not wait to retire for the night to rejoin her friend for their exhilarating romps.

To prevent her grandparents from becoming more suspicious of her behavior, Guita rose before them and removed any evidence of her excursions. She also did everything she could to show interest in her meals, although she always arrived in the dining room feeling as if she'd already partaken of the full table. While her fatigue deepened, she was able to take naps since her grandmother had taken to visiting a neighbor who was about to give birth. Mrs. Beckenhauer had long served as a midwife to the farmers in the area west of Freiburg.

"The Guttmeyers will be here later to take their daughter home," announced Mr. Beckenhauer at breakfast.

During Guita's nightly predations with Elfi, the Guttmeyers' daughter had told her she would continue to exist regardless of whether she was buried or not, but Guita was intent on preventing her interment, fearing she would never see her again.

"Please *opa*, let her stay longer in the waiting house. She is not dead," implored Guita.

"But she is, *liebling*, and she must return to her mama and papa for funeral," replied Mr. Beckenhauer, leaving the house to prepare Elfi for her ride home.

"But I have heard the bell ring each night," protested Guita.

"Impossible, my child. I removed the string from her finger two nights ago when I was certain she was gone. Now I must go."

"May I go with you to say goodbye to Elfi," pled Guita.

"No, the waiting house is no place for a living child. Please help *oma* prepare the pastry for the Guttmeyers' arrival."

"But, *opa*...!"

"Quiet, now," snapped Mr. Beckenhauer, trudging from the room.

Two hours later the Guttmeyers arrived for their daughter. They remained in their carriage until Mr. Beckenhauer greeted them and invited them into his house for tea and cake before fetching their daughter. Mrs. Guttmeyer held a handkerchief to her face and sobbed softly as they sat around the dining room table.

"I am sorry that she did not come back, *Frau* Guttmeyer, but she is with God now, and that is the better thing," said Mr. Beckenhauer, breaking the awkward silence.

"Please, *Herr* Beckenhauser, we would like to take our Elfi home now," said Mr. Guttmeyer, rising from the table.

"Of course, bring the carriage to the waiting house entrance," replied Mr. Beckenhauer. "She is ready for her final journey."

When the Guttmeyers and Beckenhauers left the house to retrieve the body, Guita followed.

As Mr. Beckenhauer opened the waiting house door they froze in shock. Standing before them in her tidy pink frock was Elfi Guttmeyer smiling—her arms outstretched to her parents.

"God has given you back to us! It's a miracle!" wailed Hadelin Guttmeyer, running to her child and embracing her.

The Beckenhauers watched the scene in disbelief. *How is it possible?* wondered Mr. Beckenhauer. He had just checked her before the Guttmeyers' arrived and she was quite dead. *Perhaps it truly is a miracle.*

"Elfi, you are back!" cried her father, wrapping his arms around his restored family.

"Hello dear mama and papa," said Elfi, turning to greet the Beckenhauers' granddaughter. "Guita, my friend…hello."

"But how do you know…?" uttered Mr. Beckenhauer.

He did not complete his inquiry. *A miracle, yes, it must be a miracle*, he concluded, although he had never put much stock in the possibility of miracles.

"Come, my treasure, we will take you home," said Mrs. Guttmeyer, still clutching her revivified daughter.

As the Guttmeyers climbed into their carriage, Elfi smiled and waved at Guita, who returned her farewell with a knowing smile.

On the ride home, swirling ribbons of decaying leaves crisscrossed the dirt road and the wind pounded the sides of the carriage in which Elfi sat between her grateful parents.

"Oh, *mein kleiner schatz*, you are cold," observed Hadelin Guttmeyer, cuddling her beloved as their carriage moved through the gloomy twilight forest.

As Elfi gazed at the coiled trail ahead, one thought took possession of her mind:

How nice it would be to see them bleed.

Ghost Boy

His colours laid so thick on every place,
as only showed the paint, but hid the face.
— John Dryden

Mbeya Road connected the village of Kisessa to the city of
Mwanza. It was a patchwork of riven asphalt and rutted soil on
which Huru Mohubi ran for his life as the moon drifted in and out of
arid clouds. The stumps of the two fingers severed by the witch
doctor's men throbbed but didn't slow his flight to Mama Lweza. If
he were caught, all of his body parts would be harvested and
marketed to bring magical powers and instant wealth to others.
Since his birth, Huru's bleached white skin had been a curse rather
than a blessing for him—it certainly brought him no good fortune.
Life as an albino had been a misery, and now at eighteen he was as
close as he'd ever come to being hacked to death because of the
color of his flesh. While the white hippo was revered for its
uniqueness, his human kind were feared and slaughtered because of
their uncommon pigmentation.

Mama Lweza had saved his life before, as she had other African
albinos, and if he could reach her, she would save him again. Her
small brick and tin hut was perched on Lake Ukerewe's edge on the
northern fringe of Tanzania's second largest municipality. Stopping
to catch his breath, Huru calculated that he must travel nine more

25

kilometers to evade the fate his would-be butchers had in mind for him. There were five of them on his trail and at one point he could see their machetes as they caught the intermittent moonbeams. To Huru, they looked like a swarm of fireflies dancing on the dark horizon. As a boy he loved to collect the flashing insects in a jar and watch them blink on and off. Like him, they too, were thought to possess magical powers, but unlike him, they were valued alive. So many times Huru wished he were a lightning bug, instead of a poor ghost boy.

"The Lord made you from fire as well. You are as the flying sparks…a shining boy of the stars. So special on this earth, my sweet child," once comforted Mama Lweza, who'd cared for Huru after his parents abandoned him, fearing him possessed of the wicked shatani spirit.

At sixteen, Huru had left Mama Lweza's care to work along side her brother Abasi in Kisessa, gathering sisal for rug makers. It was hard work, but Huru felt pride in supporting himself. Lweza's younger sibling was kind and defended him from villagers who mocked Huru when they went to market. When Darweshi, the local witch doctor, declared him the cause of a long drought, it became increasingly difficult for Huru to accompany Abasi into the center, so he would remain inside their modest hut until the older man returned. On two occasions, strangers had approached the hut while Huru was alone, but Abasi had returned in time to chase them away.

A month after the second encounter, Huru was finally abducted by the albino hunters and taken to the dwelling of Kisessa's prophet. It was there that Huru's fingers were lobbed off in order to be ground up and placed in amulets for sale to those that could afford their high price. The rest of his body would fetch millions of shillings, boasted the men who brought him to the witch doctor.

"An arm worth a hundred thousand shillings. A foot fifty thousand, brothers," happily declared one of his captors.

"Oh, but the ghost's head! It be worth three hundred thousand!"

shouted another, and they all cheered and swung their blades high in the air.

It surprised Huru that he wasn't chopped to death immediately. Instead, he was deposited in a tiny shed next to the witch doctor's house. In the suffocating heat, he removed his shirt and wrapped it around the remains of his right hand after attempting to cauterize the ragged incisions with a mixture of clay and saliva. He could hear the incantations of Darweshi and the cadenced responses of his assistance as the night deepened. Then silence followed, and Huru made his escape by tunneling under the thin Mukwa planks comprising the outbuilding. He was only a few hundred feet away when he heard voices shouting that he'd disappeared.

"Look, I see the shadow of the ghost boy!" exclaimed someone from the direction of the oracle's compound.

At once, Huru knew he was in a race for his life, and he sprinted across the dusty terrain like the Masai tribesmen he'd seen on the Serengeti. He felt he'd extended the distance between himself and his predators, only to realize they were within striking distance when he felt the sting of a rock against his bare shoulder. He left the road and zigzagged through a maze of shanties in an attempt to confuse his trackers.

"He has tricked us again with his black magic," observed one of the hunters, as Huru hid only a few feet from the group.

When they left the area, Huru set out as well, but with a newfound determination to deprive them of their prized bounty. The words of Mama Lweza rang in his ears and gave him renewed purpose.

"You may be different, but that's what makes you one of the Lord's special children."

Huru quickly recalculated his course by locating the brightest star in the turbid western sky. Unlike most albinos, his vision was unimpaired, and he used his good eyesight to his advantage all his young life. He now ran parallel to the road only using it when its shoulder became obstructed by rocks or fell away due to erosion. At his current pace, he'd reach Mama Lweza before the sun rose behind him and made it easier for Darweshi's henchmen to detect him.

Huru's heart pounded harder when he reached the rim of the great lake, which meant that he was nearing his destination. He had not sensed his pursuers in a while, and it increased his hope that he would reach Mama Lweza's shelter before they could catch him. As he moved up the hyacinth choked shoreline, two figures suddenly appeared from the brush, and when he looked behind him, there were two more figures advancing toward him. When he was about to run into the thickets, a fifth figure emerged, and he knew he was trapped. The only open route left to him was the water, and Huru couldn't swim. Still, he waded into the thick grassipes thinking he would rather drown than be hacked apart.

With each step Huru took into the lake, his stalkers moved closer to him, swinging their machetes and speaking in unison.

"No more evil ghost boy. No more devil tricks. We will take your powers."

Huru was waist deep in the water when the ground beneath his feet disappeared and he went under. He could hear the muffled voices of his foes shouting as he floated in the darkness of the cool lake.

"We cannot swim, so Great Ukerewe will take your Juju spirit."

Their banishments were replaced by sweet singing as Huru's heart stopped. On entering the sacred land of Mpemba, dozens of fellow albinos reached out for him, while Mama Lweza sang a song of exultation.

Eh Yakobo,
Eh Yakobo,
Walala?
Walala?

Amka twende Shule
Haya njoo,
Haya njoo,

After the first stanza, everyone joined in, forming a wide circle and dancing above the thin clouds that hung over the infinite savanna. Villagers entered from all directions and joined the joyous activity, kissing and hugging the young albinos. Never before had Huru felt such happiness and love.

Un-slung Hero

Well it is known that ambition can creep
as well as soar.
— Edmund Burke

After nearly nine years of teaching physics at an obscure mid-western college, Glen Myerson had nearly given up on the idea of a distinguished academic career. For the first time he was seriously considering joining his father in his insurance business, and while it held no appeal for him, at least it would get him out of the corn fields and back to the New England area that he loved. Peddling car and homeowner policies in Providence was preferable to serving as a member of a faculty for which he held little affection and respect. The coup de grace for Glen had occurred in the most recent faculty meeting when the football coach made a statement in support of the teaching staff that underscored for him just how embarrassing and pitiful things were at Noloc College and how desperately he needed to leave.

"These kids don't know how good they got it with such great professors. You guys *are* Noloc College. You're the un-slung heroes of this place. You kick their glutes to make them perform, and you got to do that because they're lazy and don't care about learning stuff. They just want to drink and go on booty calls," proclaimed Arnie Boslin during the dean's monthly conclave wherein he chided his faculty for a recent increase in the student failure rate that had caused enrollment to drop precipitously.

Coach Boslin was no friend of Dean George Carpin and he seized every opportunity to make that known to the world. No one knew for sure why the schism existed between the two men, but rumors had it that the coach's contempt for Carpin had to do with cuts in the football team's equipment budget that resulted in embarrassingly faded and worn uniforms and a curtailed travel schedule that forced the team to forfeit certain away games. Another rumor had the coach's wife sleeping with the dean, but this struck most people as unlikely since it was a widely held view that Carpin was gay.

"That's un*sung* hero, Arnie…un*sung*," corrected Dean Carpin, prompting the coach to wave him off as if he were a gnat. "And," continued Carpin, ignoring Boslin's dismissive gesture, "I would be the first to thank our good faculty for maintaining high standards, but we find ourselves in lean times, and if our numbers continue to fall it may well affect faculty salaries and even positions."

This remark caused a stir among the faculty, because like Glen most had been at the college since receiving their degrees, and, again, like Glen few had any prospects beyond the small and increasingly rundown rural campus. Once well-tended and maintained, the college campus was slowly turning shabby due to a downturn in the school's financial fortunes inspired by a number of factors, not the least being the devastating economic recession. In fact, several members of the grounds crew had been laid off since the start of the current fiscal year, and their absence was in sad evidence as the grass was left to grow higher than it should and the trash barrels were allowed to overflow. After weekends of student partying, parts of the campus looked like a third world slum.

"Not to name names, Glen, but you've done more than your share to slim down our student numbers by failing four students for plagiarism this semester alone. I'm not suggesting we turn our backs on such an egregious infraction of academic ethics, and I praise you for your rigor and high standards, but maybe a little more vetting of these kids would prevent this from happening," said Crispin with a measure of censure in the tone of his voice.

"I spend all the time I want with them," snapped Glen, shooting a look of contempt at the dean.

"Well, four students adds up to a hundred thousand dollars annually, and that's a lot of money out of the coffers. We can't let these kids leave unless there's no choice, and I don't think copying a term paper warrants their failure and dismissal."

"Stealing, *not* copying," countered Glen. "It's an act of theft to take someone's work and claim it as your own, and it does warrant failure and dismissal…academic dean."

"Be that as it may, Glen, we have to consider the practical impact of such actions, and losing sorely needed tuition and housing dollars will soon put this place under, and I think most of us here don't want to lose our jobs," replied the dean scanning the audience for approbation and receiving it in spades.

Coach Boslin was the only one in the room to side with Glen and he did so with two chunky thumbs held high and by trying to high-five Glen across a row of annoyed professors. It was he and Coach Malaprop against the world, thought Glen, who sank down into his seat and took a mental leave from the proceedings. Lately there was seldom a faculty meeting that held his attention for very long, and he would drift off within minutes of the dean calling the group to order.

* * *

Being an un-slung hero at Dry Gulch College, as Glen had come to call it, was not what he had imagined for his life. Long ago it had occurred to him that in order to get out of his career cul-de-sac he had to publish something that would catch the eye and inspire the admiration of the scientific community, and that is what he had set about to do but with little success. His work on the Supercavitation Theory published in two journals had not exactly launched him into the academic stratosphere. Now, however, he felt he might have discovered a way to jump-start his atrophying career.

For years he had been looking and praying for something that might set his work apart from the rest of the field but he never expected to come across it in his own backyard. On occasion Glen had gone through the collection of papers donated to the college by Dr. Owen Richards, an alumnus, who had achieved a degree of acclaim for his research in astronomy. In the bottom of one of three boxes crammed with notes and articles by the long-dead scholar, Glen had come across a manila envelope containing a carefully handwritten document. He removed it and read it with great curiosity. It was only on his second reading of the five-page text that it struck him that Richards had drafted a unique take on the Core Theory as applied to the formation of planets.

Wanting to spend more time with the document, Glen managed to slip it out of the library and return with it to the small apartment he had leased since separating from his wife a year earlier. Over the next several hours he poured over Richards's paper, and with each inspection he became more excited by the dead scientist's astute speculations. He had clearly been about to make a significant contribution to the field of astrophysics. A date in the corner of one of the pages revealed that Dr. Richards had been working on his hypothesis just a few days before he died, and it occurred to Glen that it was almost a certainty no one had seen the document he now held in his hands. Since the writings were over twenty years old and had never appeared in published form to the best of Glen's knowledge, he figured Richards had never revealed the nature of his final work. Surely, if anyone had been aware of the research, it would have appeared by now, reasoned Glen. It was that important.

Over the next few days, Glen searched the Internet for anything resembling Richards's novel theorems and as expected he found nothing. Indeed, the work was original in every way, and he pondered what to do with the surprising find. He knew its unearthing might benefit him, but he also knew his involvement would only constitute a footnote to Richards's groundbreaking study and not enough to make a genuine difference in his own career. He would be the rube who stumbled upon another's profound insights, not the guy who originated them, and that would mean little in the world of high science and scholarship. For all his efforts and aspirations he would remain a mere shadow figure in the panoply of academic luminaries.

Slowly entering his thoughts, however, was an idea so alien to him that it struck him at once as both absurd and disdainful. That it had even occurred to Glen caused him shame. Yet the notion kept asserting itself and deprived him of sleep until he reluctantly decided to embrace it. His soul be damned—he would claim the research as his own while giving ample credit to Richards for his initial formulations, but still essentially presenting it as his own scholarship. The material would need polishing to ready it for publication, as Richards had not been the best of writers, but editing was something Glen did well. He justified appropriating the work by convincing himself he was giving it life and in doing so honoring the memory of the late scientist. He and Richards would be collaborators…indeed, coauthors. Had he not found and rescued the piece, Richards's brilliant work would have been forever lost. In his view, he was providing an invaluable service to the field of scientific inquiry. These thoughts helped ameliorate the guilt that arose in him, especially when he was reminded of his reputation as Noloc's foremost anti-plagiarism crusader.

* * *

It took Glen a few weeks to put the Richards research into publishable form and then months passed before he heard back favorably from the prestigious journal to which he had submitted it. The day he received notice that the article would appear in what was regarded as the top scholarly venue for research in astrophysics was a day of wide-ranging emotions for Glen. On the one hand he was thrilled by its acceptance and the recognition it was about to bring him and on the other hand he was apprehensive about the possible discovery of his unscrupulous act.

Glen said nothing about the article until it appeared and when it did publish, the news of it swept the scientific field like wildfire and quickly became the buzz of the campus. Reaction by his fellow Noloc colleagues was mixed but mostly reserved, but Glen attributed this to envy. There were no superstars on faculty at the small college and his sudden notoriety clearly was a thorn in the side of those who also had harbored dreams of escaping the mundane and lackluster existence of life at the no account institution. It was a bitter pill for many of them to take and one Glen enjoyed administering.

In the weeks following the publication of the article, Glen had been the subject of considerable attention by the scholarly community and had been invited to speak in a number of conference venues. This sudden renown did not escape the attention of Dean Carpin, who had become very solicitous of Glen's surprising celebrity. A cocktail party ostensibly to mark the semester's end was really a guise to showcase Noloc's academic super nova. It was obvious to Glen that the dean wanted to exploit his newly found eminence for the benefit of the institution. The school's publicity director had been working overtime to get press in both local and national venues and had succeeded beyond anyone's expectations landing stories in *Newsweek* and the *Chronicle of Higher Education*, as well as other widely read publications.

Glen's anxiety over filching Richards's research was eclipsed by the attention he received from the academic world and the deep satisfaction he derived from the obvious jealousy it generated in many of his senior colleagues, whom he had long disliked and who had long disliked him. These were the same people who had tried without success to keep him from tenure in order to validate their narrow existences and feed their toxic agendas. However, given his handful of publications, albeit in secondary journals, he was more than qualified for the distinction. Compared to the meager research vitae of those judging him, he was a worthy candidate for promotion and the job for life that came with it. His only weakness had been his less than stellar student evaluations stemming from the rigor in his courses and his determination to root out cheaters and fail them. Though this cost him points he still managed to score above many of the old timers who were intent on doing him in. In the end, he had effectively neutralized their malicious intent, and it was something they held against him now more than ever in the wake of his achievement.

* * *

The excitement over his groundbreaking article continued into the summer as Glen learned he had been short-listed for a prize by the National Astrophysics Council. He expected all the recognition would soon result in a job offer and was making plans for his departure when he received a call from the dean to meet. It was obvious to Glen that the school was eager to retain his services but there was little it could offer to keep him. In fact, Glen had already decided to resign his position fully confident that he would soon be asked to join a major university, and even if it meant taking a semester or two off before selecting the right post, he was determined to leave Noloc right away. At the meeting, he would take the opportunity to inform the dean of his plan and that would provide him with incalculable pleasure. He had long looked forward to this day and still had trouble believing it had arrived.

Dean Carpin greeted him with considerable warmth directing him to a chair and offering him a beverage.

"Thank you for coming right over, Glen. I wanted to have a little chat with you before the paparazzi took up all of your time. How are you dealing with the tremendous attention?" asked Carpin, pouring coffee into a piece of delicate china and handing it to Glen.

"I'm dealing with it just fine. You heard about the NAC prize?" asked Glen, already certain he had.

"Yes, congrats on that. Quite the honor, and I bet you get it, too," responded the dean, settling into his seat.

"Well, it would be something," commented Glen sipping his coffee and gauging the dean's reaction.

"Yes, it would, and it would be very meaningful to Noloc as well, and that's why I wanted to talk with you, Glen. I suspect other institutions may be trying to lure you away, and I wanted to see if the college might do something to keep that from happening. We're prepared to give you your own program, and I'm sure with your growing reputation, we can generate enough funding to make it a worthwhile venture for you and the school. With your blessing, we thought we might call it The Myerson Institute of Astrophysics Inquiry, and we already have some rich alums willing to provide startup money."

"Sorry, George, but I'm leaving. This is not the place for me any more, if it ever was. I appreciate your offer, but I think I'll be happier elsewhere," replied Glen feeling something akin to euphoria.

"Would you at least consider the possibility? This could be good for you and Noloc,"

"Frankly, I think what is best for me is to leave Noloc, and I don't really care what is good for this gloomy institution, George," replied Glen rising from his seat.

"Well, Glen, I think you may want to reconsider, because, frankly, it would be better for you to accept the offer," said the dean looking at Glen intently.

"No, I will not reconsider. Goodbye, George," said Glen turning to leave.

"I know what you've done, Glen," said the dean in a tone that reminded Glen of the way his mother spoke to him when she caught him fibbing.

"What do you mean?" replied Glen trying to appear at ease but feeling otherwise.

"Your famous article is not really yours, Glen. Imagine you, the great crusader against plagiarism, stealing someone else's work. I know that research was Owen Richards's," said Crispin smugly, his thick eyebrows arching imperiously.

"What are you talking about?" replied Glen beginning to feel light-headed.

"Being a naturally curious fellow, I examined the contents of the Richards collection closely when we first received it, and I came across an envelope containing the notes on something called the Core Theory. They didn't mean much to me, of course, not being a scientist, but I certainly got an idea what was in there. Did you know I've always had a pedestrian interest in astronomy, Glen? Even minored in general science in college. When I read your article I made the connections pretty quickly because I remembered some of Richards's assertions about, what was it, 'the polarization in coupled-cluster theory'?"

Dean Carpin read from a lined pad that he held before him like a psalm book.

"Yes, I think that's what it was, right, Glen?"

"That's ridiculous. What do you know about my work? Sure, I drew on Owen's study. That's what it's there for. We all rely on existing research to take our own to the next step," refuted Glen, rubbing his sweaty palms against his trousers.

"You did a good deal more than simply draw on Richards's research, Glen. You copied the whole thing and put your name on it. You stole it just like all those students you failed. I couldn't believe it when it began to dawn on me that you had done that. Not you of all people. I was shocked."

"I'm leaving," spat Glen moving toward the door.

"I don't think so, Glen. If you do, I'll be forced to take this public, and I don't think you'll be a candidate for any award or job. On the other hand, if you agree to remain here at Noloc College, you can head your own program, and no one will ever be the wiser. Our little secret, right? It's really the best outcome, Glen, if you think about it, and I really think you'll want to think about it very seriously. Let's meet again tomorrow, okay? Have a good day," said the dean escorting Glen from his office.

* * *

When Glen returned to his apartment he found a call on his answering machine from the chair of the astronomy department at Stanford inviting him to visit. He erased the message and sat at his desk scanning the article that was about to change his life but not in the way he had dreamed it would. By the time he had left the campus he already knew he had to remain at Noloc, because the alternative was unthinkable to him. Being exposed to the world as a plagiarist was by far the worst of the two options presented to him. As time passed he conceded that his punishment was appropriate for the crime he had committed and he accepted his fate. A career in academic purgatory was the price he would have to pay for his major lapse in moral judgment.

* * *

At the modest ceremony launching the new Myerson Institute, Coach Boslin threw his arms around Glen and exuberantly announced to all within earshot that he was truly the greatest of all the college's un-slung heroes.

"Thank you," responded Glen, as graciously as his deflated pride would allow, "I don't deserve your good words."

"Of course you do," interjected Dean Carpin, patting Glen on the back. "You've earned them."

The Sick House

"Infantile paralysis empties house of family."
— *Providence Tribune,* August 4, 1953

The story about that creepy old house across the street goes something like this. Almost two years ago all the kids that lived there got polio and one, a little girl named Sara, died. This drove her parents crazy and they disappeared with their two other kids, who were crippled by the disease. No one has heard from them since, and some say they went out into Narragansett Bay on their dad's small fishing boat and drowned during a storm, but no bodies have ever been found. So the place is haunted. At least that's what I believe, and most of my friends think so, too, except Henry, who thinks that idea is a bunch of baloney. He might be right, but I don't think so.

I'm going to move my bed, because where it is now I go to sleep looking at that empty place, and I swear to God it's looking back at me. The second-floor windows are like eyes that stare at me in my attic bedroom. If I had a shade on my window, I'd pull it down. My dad is supposed to put one up but he never seems to get around to it. Sometimes I hang my clothes over the empty curtain rod but my mom says it looks bad from the street and takes them down when I forget to do it. Then I end up with nothing to keep what we call the Polio House from gawking in at me.

When I woke up in the middle of the night a couple of weeks ago

43

I saw lights on in one of the windows, and there was a shadow moving in the room. It was small and I could tell it was her…the dead girl, Sara. When I told my parents they said it was impossible, because no one lived there anymore and the electricity was shut off. They said I was just dreaming and letting my imagination go wild. My mother shrugged it off, saying I should focus on other things, like my schoolwork.

As usual my father just cursed the place, calling it a damn eyesore and complaining that it was dragging down the neighborhood, which was already on the slide because so many undesirables were moving in.

"Maybe some decent white folks will buy the place and clean it up," he said, adding that more than likely it would just go empty because it was falling apart. "Looks like it's going to topple over. It's a real blight, and with all the nutty talk about it being full of polio and haunted nobody will ever buy it, except maybe some coons. Hey, then it really will be filled with spooks," he joked, and I gave him a hard look because of my friend, Henry, being colored. "Well that's all we need living across the street from us. Maybe you'll feel differently if that happens, kiddo. Those people turn everything bad. They're like a disease."

Sometimes when it's windy the Polio House seems to wail like it's in pain and the harder the wind blows the louder and more horrible it gets. I'm not kidding, lots of times its sobbing keeps me awake late at night. Everything it does seems scarier in my room than anywhere else in the house. It's like it's chosen to bother me more than anyone else. But I'm not going to let it chase me out of my room. Even though Henry thinks the whole thing about the house is pretty stupid, he says that there's no way he would get up in the middle of the night to take a leak out of the window with that old place looking at his ding-a-ling.

Henry is one of the funniest kids I have ever known, even if my dad says I should stay away from people like him. Sometimes I think our house is just as sick as the Polio House.

My Drowning Country

Contemplate the heavens and the earth, the night and the day, the clouds and the seas, the winds and the waters...
— The Quran

The day Vivathi's beloved Auntie Ranna died the ocean began to wash over the floor of their modest dwelling. With the island flooded it was not possible to give her a proper burial, so Vivathi loaded her tiny body into their old wooden rowboat, along with a tin container of fresh water and another with rice and fish. She then set out for the nearest body of land, whose distance she did not know since the once neighboring islands were no longer within eyesight; they, too, had been devoured by the sea.

Auntie Ranna had been Vivathi's last living relative since her parents and brothers lost their lives two years earlier when the small Maldive atoll where she had lived since birth was swept by giant tidal waves that rolled across the Laccadive Sea as a result of an earthquake off the coast of India.

At the start of her journey the birds, which also had been forced to evacuate the sinking island, followed her as she rowed toward the empty horizon. The sandpipers, plovers, terns, and herons swooped and glided in the cloudless blue sky and she spoke to them as the friends they had always been. Also with her was the Bodubera her aunt had sung as Vivathi lamented the absence of a young man to court her.

"But you are only sixteen, my dearest niece," replied Auntie Ranna, who would then wrap her willowy arms around her and softly sing:

Aadha hissa mere to dil ki kahani ka tu
half my heart's story is you
Piya Mein baaki aadha
my beloved, I am another half

Poor Auntie Ranna, thought Vivathi, and tears fell from her eyes as she gazed at her motionless figure nestled in the narrow of the canoe's hull. Until now she had not noticed that her aunt clutched a pale purple orchid in her hand. The sight made Vivathi's chest heave in sorrow, because she remembered how much joy flowers gave her.

"Bread feeds the body, but flowers feed the soul," had proclaimed Auntie Ranna on more than one occasion.

Vivathi's moist eyes looked back and her gaze then settled on her nearly vanished island, which now revealed only the tops of its towering palm trees. She wondered what happened to the breadfruit, taro, and banana plants that had so richly nourished them. *Will the fish feed on them and love them as much as I did?*

She mourned the loss of the colorful geckos. The turtles would swim to land somewhere, but she doubted the skills of geckos in high waters. Vivathi wondered, too, about the survival of the cuckoo birds and the short-eared owls. Would they be able to fly to safety? She had not seen either among the flock circling overhead.

Soon, night was upon her and she watched the falling stars and scanned the dark horizon until she fell into an exhausted sleep. In her dreams she celebrated the feast of *Kuda Eid* with her lost family. Her auntie and mother sang as they prepared fried fish balls and Kira Sarbat, the sweet milk she so loved. Her father and brothers kicked around a football and chuckled when it landed on the table where the meal was being assembled.

"Silly men. You will eat this and not the Gula, if it comes this way again," chided Auntie Ranna heaving the ball back, and her remark made her father and brothers laugh even more.

* * *

She awoke as the eastern sky was turning a soft blue and kneeled for prayer. As she did her bare foot touched the cold flesh of her aunt and she pulled away quickly causing the small boat to rock violently. It was then that her aunt spoke.

"Oh, my darling Vivathi, do not fear the dead. We live in spirit without need of earthly hosts. We are as the air, strong and everywhere."

Vivathi stared at her aunt's motionless lips now as pale as her face, and for the first time she noticed a pungent odor coming from her.

"The body turns to guano when the spirit leaves it. It is good for feeding the creatures of the deep. You must remove me from the canoe, but I will remain with you forever," said Auntie Ranna in a near whisper.

"Dear Auntie, I cannot do as you ask. I must take you to land and bury you properly," replied Vivathi, fighting back tears.

"That is not necessary, my child. The sea is no different than the soil. In either the body rejoins the cycle of energy. In its passing it sustains the living and in doing so returns to the realm of life itself."

Vivathi knew she must do as her aunt requested, and it was with a heavy heart that she rolled the rigid body into the sea.

"I love you, my child," said Auntie Ranna as she disappeared into the emerald brine that reached the four horizons.

"I love you, too, Auntie," replied Vivathi feeling more alone than ever before.

* * *

For the rest of the day, Vivathi rowed in the direction of the gulls hoping they would lead her to land, but none was to be found. Still she remained hopeful of finding shore even as the sun began to burn her skin and cause her discomfort. By nightfall her face and arms felt on fire and she was thankful for the sun's departure and the cooling breezes that followed.

Once again she dreamed of her family and the wonderful moments they shared, such as when her brothers rode her on their backs and her mother made her a beautiful sari that she wore to the *Eid ul-Al'h'aa* Festival. Even in her sleep she smiled from the joy these images gave her, but in one dream she saw the on-rushing wave that took away her loved ones and she awoke crying.

* * *

On the third day at sea Vivathi's food and water supply was gone, as were the gulls she had been following. The sea was like glass with not a single ripple disturbing its varnished surface. There was no movement of any sort to be seen. Even the oars did not churn the liquid they cleaved. It was as if the earth and all the elements it possessed were frozen in a photograph.

Throughout the day Vivathi's mind played other tricks on her. She saw men perform the *Dhandi Jehun* revels around her boat. They were replaced by a group of women dancing and singing the Thaara and children frolicking across the water in spirited games. These phantasms deflected the reality of her desperate situation and lifted her spirits for the time they lasted.

It was a deafening crack of thunder that broke the solace of Vivathi's happy illusions. The sky was now black as pitch and the sea climbed and dropped in giant swells. The rowboat lurched and Vivathi prayed while clinging to its sides.

"You will endure," declared Auntie Ranna's voice from within the gales blowing so hard Vivathi could not sit up. "You will endure, my niece."

"Auntie, help!" Vivathi pleaded as the boat tipped but then steadied despite the surging water.

The strong wind still kept Vivathi from rising to see what was happening, but she could tell the boat was moving quickly and that something was carrying it.

"*Auntie!*" Vivathi shouted, and her summons was answered by the sweet familiar laughter of her former guardian and protector.

* * *

Soon the storm abated and the sea calmed. The late day sun returned and Vivathi was able to sit upright. *What saved me?* she wondered. She looked over the side of the rowboat to find a vast winged creature swimming away. She knew from the stories her father had told her when she was little that it was the Manta Ray. In his vivid accounts, it had saved many people from certain death.

"The great *Havamasa* is a friend of man and even saves pretty little girls, too," joked Vivathi's father as he regaled her with wondrous tales about the Manta Ray before she went to sleep for the night. "It carries shipwrecked people on its broad wings. It is very strong and most kind."

"Thank you, Manta Ray," she whispered at its vanishing shadow.

* * *

The late day turned to night and then dawn arrived again bringing with it the hot sun. Vivathi's strength had drained from her and her heart's rhythm had slowed. Still she fixed her stare on the horizon for any evidence of land, but it seemed as if the earth had become only water.

"Dear Auntie, I cannot endure as you said. There is no land to give me life, so I shall perish."

As the last air streamed from Vivathi's lungs, her Auntie Ranna rose from the sea on the back of the Manta Ray.

"You will endure, my dearest child. Come join me for we shall go to the most wonderful island of all."

Vivathi's aunt lifted her limp body from the rowboat and held her close as the Manta Ray carried them away. Soon Vivathi felt her strength restored and her mood transformed. As they moved swiftly across the surface of the rising sea, they became one with the sky and Auntie Ranna sang.

> *Ishq Haaye Baithe bithaye*
> *this love, just like that*
> *Jannat dikhaye haan*
> *showed me heaven, oh yes*
> *O raama*
> *O God*

Robin on Air

And through the trembling air, sweet breathing.
— Edmund Spenser

Robin Cormier was eleven-and-a-half at the time of his death, and his doting parents were understandably devastated. The despair over the unthinkable loss of her only child nearly claimed Robin's mother Mary. For months she was inconsolable and all but beyond the effects of several different antidepressants prescribed by the family doctor. At one point it was suggested she be admitted to a local mental health facility, for fear she might do herself harm. Don Cormier was of little help to his despairing wife as he, too, felt as if his world had been dismantled. The freakish nature of the accident that took their beloved son's life compounded their anguish.

At an early age, Robin had become a shortwave radio enthusiast, much as his father had at a similar point in his youth. However, Robin's fascination with searching for long distance signals had far exceeded his father's. When most kids his age were engaged in the sports and games of childhood, Robin spent endless hours in his room tuning far away stations on the Grundig 960 classic receiver he had inherited from his father.

It was not the best shortwave radio on the market admitted Robin's father when he dug it out of a dusty storage box in the attic and presented it to his son.

"A Watkins-Johnson can draw signals from anywhere, but this old Grundig isn't bad," said Don, carefully wiping the patina of years off the set's dial and knobs with a rag dampened with isopropyl alcohol and then lugging it to Robin's room.

After settling on a suitable location for the bulky receiver, Don connected a piece of copper wire to it and strung it out of a window a couple of feet to serve as a temporary antenna.

"That should work pretty well for the time being. We'll run it over to the utility pole when I get a chance, and that will greatly strengthen the distant signals," said Don, hitting the power switch on the old Grundig, which took a while to fire up. "The tubes have to get warm before you hear anything. No solid state circuitry or transistors in this baby."

In about a minute, the Grundig was emitting loud static, and that excited both of them prompting them to hug each other.

"Great! The power supply is working. Now let's see if we can find something."

All afternoon, they scanned the multiple shortwave bands picking up exotic signals from as far away as Europe and South America. With its short antenna, the Grundig could not draw frequencies from Asia and the Pacific islands.

"When we get it out there to the pole, you'll be able to get most any place," promised Don, to the further enthusiasm of his son, whose heart jumped at the prospect of hearing voices from the other side of the world, speaking in places he hoped to someday visit.

It didn't matter to Robin that he couldn't understand the foreign chatter pouring from the large internal speakers. The very idea that he had the globe at his fingertips thrilled him, and he looked forward to stretching the antenna wire to the utility pole so that he could access countries in the farthest reaches of the planet, lands that existed in his dreams.

As the days passed Robin became a true shortwave devotee. He would spend every available minute slowly twisting the radio's tuning knob in search of another strange and curious language. When he could determine the name of the station and frequency he had picked up, he would carefully log it into his notebook. Soon page after page was filled with signals from places he didn't even know existed. On a world atlas tacked to the wall next to his treasured Grundig, he ceremoniously marked the origin of every far away frequency, his father assisting him when he could not find a particular locale. After a couple of weeks he had DX'd dozens of stations in Europe, Africa, and South and Central America, and his desire to reach more distant continents was growing quickly.

He reminded his father about his promise to stretch the antenna wire to the light pole, but Don's days at work had become all-consuming as sales quotas at the appliance store he ran had to be met by the fast-approaching close of the calendar year.

"Maybe next week," replied his father, when Robin twice broached the subject. "Definitely the week after at the latest, son."

But Robin grew impatient with the delay and decided to take action into his own hands and string the antenna wire to the utility pole when his parents were out. This involved dragging his father's metal extension ladder from the garage to the pole and climbing it to make the necessary connection.

As he ascended the ladder it struck him that by joining the receiver's antenna wire with the power line he would have vastly improved reach. He might even catch signals from airplanes, maybe even satellites. It was difficult getting to the line but by standing on top of the ladder he managed to reach it. There he draped the antenna wire over the power line and to insure a secure connection he tightly knotted it.

It was then that the copper wire of the antenna made contact with the hot cable inside the desiccated sheathing of the power line and Robin was electrocuted. The boy's lifeless body was first noticed by an elderly neighbor who had looked out of a window when the lights in her house flickered. At that moment the world of Don and Mary Cormier also went dark.

* * *

Living just yards from the site of their son's fiery demise was too much for the Cormiers, even with the drapes in the living room tightly drawn to block the utility pole their son had climbed in an effort to expand the universe of his cherished shortwave radio. To avoid encountering the site of their son's grisly death they began to enter the garage from the side door and take a quick left out of the driveway leaving the power pole receding in the opposite direction. Neither would look through the rear view mirrors of the car until long after executing a turn at the corner of the block, and even then they were reluctant to look for fear the pole had followed them like some grotesque predator.

Shortly after his son's death, Don had made the tactical error of glimpsing out of his bedroom window, which faced the street. In that fraction of a second his stare had fixed on the stain on the sidewalk left by his son's shattered body. It sent icy shudders through him and a sense of remorse so deep he thought he would implode.

There was no doubt in his mind that he had caused his son's death by putting off what he had promised, and his guilt haunted him. Had he strung the goddamn antenna wire to the pole as he had pledged, Robin would be alive and life would not be the hell it now was for him and his wife.

Don knew Mary blamed him for their son's tragic end. He could tell by the look in her eyes that she considered him Robin's murderer. He was relieved that she had not actually verbalized her feelings, because if she had he felt he would do something desperate. What exactly, he did not know, but to be accused of his son's death by the woman he deeply loved would be too much to bear, and some act of contrition would be necessary. At the very least he would have to leave, go somewhere and hide for the balance of his pitiable existence. Perhaps he would climb the same pole his son did and in revenge and repentance drive a knife into the power line that had so savagely taken his boy's life. It would be a way to deal with his own anger and remorse, but what effect would it have on his wife? No doubt he would be responsible for a second and perhaps fatal blow to her tenuous existence.

* * *

The weeks dragged on in unrelenting gloom, Don going to work and remaining locked in his office to avoid contact with his fellow workers and Mary in self-exile at home for the same reason. Conversation between the two had dwindled to an occasional monosyllable, mainly "yes" and "no." They no longer shared the same bed and only rarely sat in the same room together. They were becoming strangers in their shared grief.

The day they would have celebrated Robin's twelfth birthday was the hardest for them since his death. Mary wept all day in her bedroom and Don took to his basement workroom where he sat in the dark until the iridescent digits on his watch revealed it was close to midnight. He then slipped under the blankets on the living room couch where he had been sleeping lately and drifted into a fitful sleep in which he climbed the deadly utility pole in a vain effort to prevent his son's detonation. This recurring nightmare always woke him and left him feeling even more forlorn, if that were possible.

But on this night as he lay in the dark he heard an odd noise coming from the direction of his dead son's room. He rose and slowly moved down the hall toward the crackling and hissing sound and as he approached Robin's room he realized it was the sound of static like that made by a radio. His heart began to pound as he opened the door to his son's bedroom, which he hadn't entered since his death. In the darkness glowed the dial of the Grundig 960. Deep inside the static he detected what he thought was a voice, and he moved the tuning knob to sharpen the reception. What he heard sucked the breath from his lungs.

"This is Robin Cormier on frequency 11.855 megahertz. Can you hear me, Dad? I'm at the southern tip of New Guinea facing the Coral Sea Basin. It's so beautiful. I wish you were here."

Then the transmission ceased, leaving Don stunned and shaken.

"Oh my, God!" he finally blurted and ran to tell Mary. "Open up!" he shouted as he banged on the bedroom door. "You won't believe who I heard. Robin, our son! Sweet Jesus!"

"What are you talking about?" said his wife as she warily opened the door. "What are you harping about? Have you gone crazy? Don't say such things!"

"I swear I heard Robin on the Grundig. He's in New Guinea," replied Don, tears flowing down his cheeks.

Mary felt a trace of the long dormant affection she had for her husband return as he stood before her weeping.

"It was him on the radio, and he sounded fine. He asked if I could hear him and that it was beautiful where he was. He seemed happy."

"Look, come in and get some sleep. You're overtired and hearing things" said Mary, but as she was about to lead her husband to their bed loud static came from Robin's room.

"It's him. It's Robin," shouted Don grabbing her arm and leading her to the source of the scratchy sound.

"No, I don't want to go in there, Don! Let me go!" yelled Mary but he dragged her into the room despite her protests.

"*Shhh*, listen, I'm going to get our son," said Don twisting the tuning dial on the big radio as Mary tried to break his grip.

"This is Robin Cormier on frequency 13.870 in Romania. Can you hear me, Mom and Dad? It's so beautiful here…"

Mary shrieked when she heard her son's voice and fell to the floor sobbing.

"You see, I told you I heard him. It's really Robin. It's really him."

Every night thereafter they listened to their son as he broadcast from all over the world.

"This is Robin Cormier on frequency 15.345 in Argentina... This is Robin Cormier on frequency 99.995 in Egypt... This is Robin Cormier on frequency 12.085 in Mongolia..."

The deep wounds that had afflicted their hearts disappeared into the sweet air.

Property Values

Property has its duties as well as its rights.
— Thomas Drummond

Sally Girard was killed in the early morning hours of June 14th, when she ran a stop sign while texting a friend and was hit broadside by a truck. Angie Harrington, whose husband had also died recently, was jolted from sleep by the sound of the crash. Her house had the misfortune of being located at the most dangerous intersection in town and as a result Angie had become somewhat inured to the frequent late night squeal of rubber on asphalt and the deep thud of large moving objects colliding into each other. From the sound of this one, she knew the cars' occupants were in serious trouble, so she promptly dialed 911 while looking out of her bedroom window that faced the notorious junction.

From her vantage point and with the help of a solitary streetlight Angie could make out a body on the pavement. Whoever it was had not worn a seatbelt, concluded Angie, who then closed the curtains to block out the grisly scene. Within minutes she heard the inevitable sirens, and shortly after that the flashing lights of the ambulance and police cars seeped through the thick fabric of her window dressings. This was an all too familiar scenario to Angie, and she was more anxious than ever to sell her house. During the time they lived in it, Angie and her husband experienced a half-dozen crashes of varying severity, and even before he died they had put the house on the market, no longer willing to tolerate these invasions of their peace.

* * *

When the accident was finally cleared away, Angie tried to go back to sleep, but as was the case on so many other occasions, that was difficult due to her frayed nerves and the disturbing accident images that kept asserting themselves. In the morning, she contacted her Realtor and lowered the price she had been asking for her house. At this point, all she wanted out of the sale was enough to purchase a small condo at the nearby shore. Her late husband's modest investments would allow her to live comfortably if not lavishly and she was close to drawing social security, which would get her through her so-called golden years.

An open house was slated for the weekend, and Angie's Realtor felt optimistic that the new asking price would result in an offer. The morning of the open house, Angie rose early to make sure her yard was free of any signs of last night's accident or the usual trash tossed on it by passing cars. Beer cans were the items she usually found, but to her surprise there were none. In fact, the area was free of all debris except for a mound of rocks that held a framed photograph of a young woman, and Angie quickly realized that the bereaved relatives of the night's car crash victim had erected a monument for their lost loved one. Although moved by the sight of the makeshift memorial, she remembered it was the day of her open house and her heart sunk. A tombstone in front of her house would not be a selling point, she reflected, as she began to dismantle it.

While she was removing the mound of rocks one by one, a car pulled up and a middle-aged couple carrying flowers climbed out shouting for her to stop.

"What!" exclaimed Angie startled by the sudden interruption.

"Hey, what are you doing? That's for our daughter who just died here," replied the distraught man approaching her.

"Please, leave it alone," added the woman accompanying him.

"I'm sorry, but I can't have this here. I feel terrible about what happened, but it can't stay. I'm trying to sell my house, and this would turn people off," Angie responded handing them their dead daughter's photograph.

"It's just for a while until her friends have a chance to pay their respects and visit where she died," pleaded the man on the verge of tears.

"You can't do this," implored the woman clasping her hands as if to pray.

"But I have a lot of people coming here today, and if this is here, it will be a major turnoff. I'm sorry...really," replied Angie turning to return to her house.

"Oh my, God! Look! Look!" blurted the woman as Angie walked away. "She's crying. There's a tear coming from her eye, Tom."

"Sweet Jesus, there is," answered her husband.

"Look, ma'am! Mrs. Harrington, right? Please...please take a look at this," cried out Mrs. Girard trailing Angie with the photograph.

It did, indeed, appear as if the young woman in the picture was shedding a tear, and that stopped Angie in her tracks.

"It's probably morning dew or condensation," countered Angie, giving the picture a closer look.

"No...no, it's not. When I first saw it, I wiped it away, and it came back right away."

Angie rubbed the droplet from the picture with the palm of her hand and within moments another reappeared in the dead girl's eye.

"See, it's a miracle. My little girl is communicating with us," said the woman, and Angie was at a loss for an explanation to refute the mother's seemingly outlandish claim and too exasperated to try.

"Please put it back. I know it's what Sally wants. She needs to say goodbye to her friends from where she was last alive," begged Mr. Girard.

"Okay," answered Angie moved by the distraught parents and nonplussed by the weeping photo.

What if this terrible tragedy had occurred to me? mused Angie as she returned to her house. She had always wanted a child but it wasn't in the cards and that had left her with a hole in her life that nothing else was capable of filling. It had become a permanent sadness for both her and her deceased husband, and it had cast a shadow on their otherwise salutary marriage.

* * *

For the balance of the day and well into the night, people gathered around the pile of rocks in Angie's front yard. It was long after sunset when the last person left and Angie went to bed, but again she could not get to sleep. She tossed and turned for over an hour and then gave up on the idea and tried to read but could not concentrate because her thoughts kept returning to the bizarre photograph of Sally Girard. Was it still weeping, she wondered, and put on her slippers and robe to check it out. With a flashlight in hand, Angie went to the mound and cast the beam on the picture. A tear formed in Sally's eye and ran down her cheek to the bottom of the frame where it leaked out and dropped to the ground. At the spot where it landed small flowers were sprouting from the soil. As far as Angie could recall they had not been there before the memorial was built, and it confused and disturbed her, because she was a lifelong doubter in things spiritual or paranormal in nature.

Angie stood at the monument until she heard a car moving up the road, and then she retreated to her house not wanting to be spied on in her nightclothes. Eventually she got to sleep and when she awoke she was startled to find it was late morning. As she slowly rose from bed she heard a commotion coming from outside and went to the window. On first glimpse she thought she was still dreaming. At least a hundred people occupied her front yard.

"This is ridiculous. Miracle or not, this has got to stop," she mumbled throwing on her clothes.

On her way to the door her phone rang. It was her Realtor, reporting that the mob was causing her property value to plunge faster than Fanny Mae stock.

"It was bad enough that all those accidents happened at your house, but with this I'll never be able to sell it, Angie. If you can't get them to take down that thing, you should call the police. They're trespassing, and that's illegal."

Angie said she was well aware of the situation and had told the Girards that they had until Monday to remove their daughter's monument.

"You know, there's actually something weird going on out there. The picture looks like it's crying," commented Angie, and her Realtor replied that it was a bunch of silliness.

"I don't know. I saw it myself," replied Angie, wondering if she, too, had been smitten by the hysteria.

"You can see anything you want to see, but it's a gimmick. There's something in the frame. You can buy those things on the Internet. Shit, you can buy anything on the Internet."

Angie repeated that it would be gone by Monday to which her Realtor added that if it wasn't she could not continue to list the house.

"I don't want my 'for sale' sign on some wacky impromptu shrine. It's bad for my business, and things are tough enough. When you lose your credibility, you're done."

Angie remained inside all day as the crowd continued to swell. At one point the police called and said that neighbors were complaining about uproar, and when she explained what was going on, she was advised to hire a police detail to manage the throng.

"If something happens, and that's a dangerous intersection to begin with, you'll be held responsible," she was told and reluctantly heeded the advice.

A squad car with its blue lights flashing parked in front of her house for the rest of the day. When the crowd thinned down close to midnight, the police car departed. Not long after, the handful of visitors remaining at the site left as well. As Angie had done the night before she slipped down to the monument in her robe but this time took Sally Girard's picture back to her house determined to check the frame for any tear-generating devices. She carefully dismantled the frame and closely inspected its pieces. There was no sign that anything had been tampered with, but the tears continued to form in the dead girl's eyes. Angie stood gazing down at the weeping photograph and chills ran down her back causing her to shiver. *This can't be happening*, she thought, and quickly reassembled the picture and returned it to its improvised altar. She then climbed under the covers and waited out the long night.

* * *

Throughout the morning, the crowds thickened and Angie was forced to hire police supervision again. By early afternoon, the Girards had arrived to enthusiastic fanfare from the group, and Angie bolted from her house to read the riot act to them.

"Look, you said you'd remove this stuff from my lawn by today. You're trespassing and I can have the police arrest you. I know this is important to you and, again, I'm sorry for your loss. I can only imagine how terrible this is for you, but I have a life to live, too, and it requires I sell the place, so take your daughter's picture and all those things on the rocks and leave," demanded Angie as the crowd tightened around her.

"This is a sacred site, lady. It's hallowed ground, and it cannot be violated," shouted someone behind her, and the assemblage voiced its approval.

"Leave it alone. It's not bothering anyone," shouted another member of the cabal, whose sentiments were echoed by yet another and another until the entire group was chanting, "Leave it alone...leave it alone!"

Angie was unnerved by the crowd's zeal and returned to her house fearing for her safety. She felt trapped by the situation and could see no option other than to wait it out. If she had everyone removed by the authorities, it could have serious additional repercussions for her, she feared. There was no telling what might happen given the Girards' strong feelings and those of their exuberant supporters.

As she had the last couple of days, she sequestered herself in her house to avoid the absurd and annoying scene, but it was impossible to ward off the rumble of the noise it produced and the beams of vehicle headlights in the evening, which invaded every room no matter how she tried to block them. As the day and then the night dragged on Angie found herself slipping into an even deeper funk thinking about what was happening and how it was reducing the chances of her realizing a better life. With the weight of events pressing down hard on her, she took to her bed earlier than usual but again lay awake for hours before finally achieving solace in unconsciousness.

* * *

It was at precisely the hour that Sally Girard had met her untimely demise that Angie was jerked from sleep by a horrific explosion. Her eyes first landed on the luminous red digits of the clock next to which she placed her glasses. She threw them on, nearly poking out one of her eyes, and ran to the window cracking the drapes enough to view where the sound originated. A large truck had struck the memorial and scattered it across the road. It stopped for a moment and then sped away, and Angie tried in vain to read the license plate, but all she could determine was that it was registered in state.

Again, as so many times before, she put on her robe and made her way to the cursed intersection. The stones of the monument and its adornments had been cast as far as her eyes could see. Angie walked the area looking for Sally Girard's photograph and was about to give up the search, when she spotted it in a clump of bushes. Amazingly it appeared undamaged. After pushing several rocks from the road with her feet to prevent another traffic mishap, she returned to her house with the picture, hoping that if she hid it from its crazed devotees maybe they would leave and she could get on with her existence. It was what she wanted more than anything.

* * *

What Angie hoped would happen, did. After a few days of scouring the area in vain for the photograph, the Girards and their dead daughter's adherents quit the location, and life as Angie had known it gradually returned. A month later, she agreed to an offer on her house that was considerably under what it had listed for, but she had calculated it would allow her to purchase a tiny cottage a couple of blocks away from her beloved shore. It was a compromise but one she was happy and relieved to accept.

By early fall, Angie was settled in her new home and was happy as she had been for a long time. Prior to moving, she had considered disposing of the photograph of Sally Girard once and for all, but she found she could not do it, so she brought it along to her new residence and stored it away in a trunk. It had stopped weeping, and Angie began to question whether it ever had. Over time, she found that her curiosity and interest in it grew, and on occasion she would take it out and stare at it wondering about the young life that had come to its end so soon and so violently. Her feelings for the dead girl increased as the years passed to where she had removed the picture from the trunk and placed it on the mantle above her small fireplace. Its presence gave her a feeling of comfort she had not experienced since her husband was alive.

On a balmy Spring day in early May, as Angie placed a vase of just picked daffodils on the fireplace mantle next to Sally's photograph, she noticed the long-absent tears had returned, and she took them as a sign of affirmation and love. The young woman in the picture had become a substitute for the child Angie had always longed for but never had. She would talk to the photograph for hours, and as the days and years slipped by, it began to talk to her. In time a relationship developed equal to any between a parent and its offspring.

* * *

A decade after Angie moved into her small cottage, her doctor informed her that her health was failing due to congenital heart disease, so she set about the task of preparing for her end. At first she considered being buried with the photo of her adopted child but then decided that it should be returned to its rightful owners. Though it would be painful to give up Sally's beloved image, Angie's conscience insisted she do so.

When she knew death was at her doorstep, she placed the picture in a box for mailing to the Girards the next day, but as fate would have it, that night her heart gave out. With no known relatives or existing will her estate was eventually auctioned off by the state. Weeks later, the buyer of Angie's earthly possessions discarded everything he considered of little value, including the streak stained photograph of an unknown young woman.

Drop Box

The reward of a thing done well is to have done it.
—Ralph Waldo Emerson

In his long years of emptying donation drop boxes for Goodwill, Kyle Sloan had come across some pretty strange and gross things, including dead animals, manikin limbs, dirty diapers, hypodermic needles, pornographic magazines, and even a fully-cooked turkey (still warm), to name just a few. He expected that one day he might discover a human corpse and so always approached the boxes with a certain degree of trepidation as well as curiosity. In fact, Kyle had taken to carrying a stick to probe through the contents of the containers. This practice began the same day he had encountered the entrails of a rotting raccoon in the dark recesses of a drop box. He cursed his stupidity since the smell alone should have alerted him to something foul.

Although he liked his work Kyle sometimes thought about finding other employment, but his disabled mother, knowing of his limited skill-set and compromised intellectual capacity, always discouraged his leaving Goodwill. Early in his life Kyle had been plagued by an assortment of ills leaving him unable to function on a level with most other adults. His condition had kept him from excelling in school and graduating, and it wasn't until Goodwill had trained him to drive a small truck that he had gainful employment.

Despite his reservations about his job, Kyle's outlook on life could best be described as optimistic. The idea that people would donate clothing to help the poor far exceeded his displeasure with the occasional inappropriate object left in a drop box. He attributed it to the foolishness of youth and not to actions of a truly malevolent force. *These are just kids playing a stupid joke*, he would tell himself when fishing out a stinking carcass or moldy pizza from the packed container. What *did* raise his ire was the fact that the prank often forced the disposal of what had been so generously contributed and might otherwise be useful. On occasion Kyle salvaged contaminated clothing by taking it home and washing it.

"Honey, that's very kind of you," his mother would say, adding, "You have a big heart, and I'm lucky to have a son like you. Your father would be so proud."

Kyle had just turned ten when his father died of a heart attack. Nearly two decades later, his deceased social-worker dad continued to serve as a role model inspiring him to behave kindly to all people—even those who treated him with contempt, like Sal Wheaton, a fellow drop box driver. Since Kyle had scolded him for taking things from the collections for his own benefit, Sal had treated him with ridicule, calling him a mama's boy, along with other insulting epithets. This disturbed Kyle, but since it was not in his nature to retaliate or be vindictive, he ignored Sal as best he could, steering clear of him as much as possible. His poor relationship with Sal was the only blip on the screen of his placid existence...until late one Tuesday afternoon.

It was during a drop box pick up at Tenth and Carver that things suddenly took a strange, and to Kyle, exhilarating turn. As he was loading plastic trash bags filled with used clothing into his truck an envelope with his name on it fell to the ground. He finished emptying the drop box before opening it and then its one line message baffled him.

Decide what you want and go for it

The platitude was followed by the number twelve, which further aroused his curiosity. While he appreciated the sentiment in the words, he had no clue what the number meant. He wondered who would write the message and place it in the drop-box—who knew his name and that *he* would empty that box? After reading it a couple more times, he folded the note carefully placing it in his pocket with the intention of discussing it with his mother after work. When he did show it to her, she concluded that whoever sent it to him had a benevolent objective.

"Someone is trying to give you encouragement. It may even be divine guidance. A message from a higher authority," responded Mrs. Sloan.

"But what about the number? What does it mean?" asked Kyle, staring at the missive.

"Well, you were born on the twelfth, weren't you? That makes me think it's from…you know who," replied Kyle's mother, directing her eyes upward.

Although the notion that God had sent him a message thrilled Kyle, deep down he doubted that was the case. Yet he had no idea who would be taking such a special interest in him.

"Maybe you'll get another," speculated his mother with excitement, and sure enough the next day he did.

The secret of getting ahead is getting started.

The number fifteen followed it. Again, Kyle took pleasure in the message but was perplexed by the meaning of the number along with the fact that he had no idea who was sending them to him. *Maybe it is God*, he thought, as he drove to his next pick up.

"Yes, it has to be from above," proclaimed his mother when he showed her the mysterious missive.

* * *

The next morning he told his fellow drivers about the drop box notes, and they speculated about the identity of the sender.

"Guess you have a secret admirer, Kyle. Maybe a pretty lady," said Jim Lehigh, one of his best friends at Goodwill.

"They kind of sound like the slips you get inside fortune cookies, man. Maybe there's a Chinese restaurant opening and this is the way they're promoting it," commented Billy Morgan, who Kyle liked except for his occasionally weird outlook on things.

"I think Jim may be right. Someone definitely has an eye on you," added Sal. His benign statement surprised Kyle—it had been a month since Sal had said anything to him, so he took this as a sign that Sal was overcoming his anger at him.

"My mother thinks they're messages from above," said Kyle.

"Or maybe below," replied Billy, pointing toward the ground and chuckling.

"No, I think it's all good," responded Jim, winking at Kyle, who waved and headed for his truck.

"Yeah, that's probably true," said Billy, adding his own wink.

* * *

That day as he made his rounds to the dozen drop boxes assigned to him he thought about the messages and became more convinced that his mother was right about them. They had to be from God, because he had always spoken to him about things on his mind and prayed to him to make life better. He had prayed hard for his mother who had recently lost the ability to walk due to MS, and for just as long he had been saving to buy her an electric wheelchair, though he'd only been able to save about half what it cost. Money had been tight as far back as he could remember, and there was little left after paying for life's necessities.

It was at the eighth drop box that day that Kyle came across another envelope, which he excitedly opened. What it said caused Kyle to reread it twice to gain its full import.

A journey of a thousand miles begins with a single step.

The number that accompanied it was nineteen, not one Kyle could make any connection with. His mother's birthday was on the twenty-sixth and his father's had been on the third. Nineteen meant nothing to him, yet he sensed the numbers had a purpose.

* * *

It was in the very first drop box the next day that Kyle came across another envelope, whose message greatly bolstered his spirits for the balance of his route.

You are talented in many ways.

Again, he could make no connection with the number that accompanied it. Five was only two numbers removed from his father's birthday, but that was as near as he could get to linking the figure with anything in his life.

Two days passed before Kyle found another envelope and its message was different than any of the others because it started with the number eighteen and was followed by directions.

Match the numbers you have received to the letters in the alphabet, and you will know the meaning of your life.

For the rest of his route he tried to match the numbers with the letters but had difficulty doing so. He needed to actually see the alphabet to figure it out, and he would also recruit his mother for assistance.

* * *

As soon as he arrived home, his mother noted his excitement and correctly deduced that he had received another divine message.

"This one's different, Mom. It wants me to do a puzzle," informed Kyle.

"What kind of puzzle, honey?"

"It wants the numbers to be connected with the alphabet?"

"Oh, like an code," responded his mother.

"What's that?" asked Kyle, as his mother read the message.

"It's like connecting two different things to come up with an answer to a secret," she replied, writing all the numbers from the messages on a piece of paper. "Now let's see what all this means."

Kyle sat next to her and anxiously watched as she unraveled the mystery.

"Okay, number twelve matches with an 'L.' Number fifteen mates with an 'O'. Let's see now, number nineteen is an 'S' and number five is 'E.' And the last number connects with an 'R.' So then put them together and you have L-O-S-E-R."

"Loser!" exclaimed Kyle. "Are you sure? God thinks I'm a loser?"

"Oh, honey, maybe I made a mistake. Let me do it again." And she did, but with the same result. "I'm sorry. I think someone has played a very nasty prank on you and you can be sure it wasn't God. Only humans can be so cruel."

* * *

That night Kyle went to bed earlier than usual, and in the morning he went to work feeling very down and confused. *Why did this happen to me?* He could not come up with an answer. Jim and Billy noticed his gloom and asked what was troubling him, and he told them that all the mysterious numbers had formed the word "loser." While they tried to console him, Sal laughed hysterically all the way to his truck. When he departed Jim said he thought Sal was behind the hoax, though despite his past Kyle found that hard to accept.

"He's a jerk, and I wouldn't be surprised if he did it," added Billy.

"Hey, maybe you should play the Lotto with those numbers," suggested Jim. "It's not a big jackpot, around a million bucks."

"Yeah, the drawing is tonight," added Billy, telling Kyle to buy a ticket using the numbers in all the messages.

As the day went on, Kyle came to the conclusion that it was likely Sal who had concocted the hateful scheme against him. After returning his truck for the day, Kyle headed home and on the way he took his friends' advice and bought a Lotto ticket at the convenience store near his house.

* * *

After supper Kyle and his mother took up their usual positions in front of the television to watch *Wheel of Fortune*, which not coincidentally was followed by the lottery drawing.

"Okay, get ready," urged his mother, who held the ticket containing the numbers that spelled "loser."

As the balls rolled inside the tumbler, Kyle's mother became more excited, although he felt only slight interest in the scene before him. The first ball rolled into place and it was twelve causing his mother to shriek. The next ball to fall into place was a fifteen, and Kyle's interest suddenly increased. When the third number was nineteen, they both squealed and when the fourth ball was five, they knew something extraordinary was taking place.

75

"Oh, sweet Lord!" cried Kyle's mother. "It's happening, honey! It's really happening!"

"Now for the final number in today's Lotto Sweepstakes," announced the pretty blond spinning the tumbler.

Kyle and his mother leaned into the television and clutched each other's hands.

"And the last number for 1.2 million dollars is...eighteen," proclaimed the Lotto host.

"*See!!*" screamed Kyle's mother. "The good lord was watching out for you."

"We can get you an electric wheelchair, Mom," replied Kyle hugging his mother, "and go to Florida."

They had long dreamed of visiting the Sunshine State.

* * *

The next day Kyle and his mother went to the Lotto office and claimed their prize, which was presented to them in the form of a certified check. From there they went directly to the bank where Kyle deposited half the check in his mother's account and the other in his. The balance of the day they spent shopping for an electric wheelchair and visiting a travel agency where they looked through stacks of brochures on Florida.

* * *

The following morning Kyle returned to work and on the way withdrew two thousand dollars from an ATM.

When he arrived at work and announced his win, his fellow truck drivers gathered around him enthusiastically.

"Then what are you doing here, Kyle? You're a rich man!" said Jim, patting him on the back.

"Maybe you came in to give your notice, eh?" asked Billy, wrapping his arm around Kyle's shoulder.

"No, I like my job and I'm not going to quit," responded Kyle.

"Good going, man. Wow, all that dough," said Sal.

"I got something for you," announced Kyle and then handed Jim and Billy a thousand dollars each.

"You don't have to do that, Kyle. Wow! That's really generous!" beamed Jim, and Billy just shook his head in happy disbelief.

"Hey, what about me?" asked Sal, dejectedly.

"Nothing for you," replied Kyle coldly, adding, "So who's the big "L-O-S-E-R now?"

Kyle then climbed into his truck eager to begin his day's pick ups. Six months later, the Sloans moved to Florida where Kyle joined a Goodwill Store supervising the emptying of drop boxes near the Magic Kingdom.

The Burning Turtle

The Creature has a purpose
and his eyes are bright with it.
— John Keats

Turtles communicate mostly by grunting and what they have to say is amazing. I know, because one has spoken to me since I was nine. At first I didn't understand it, but as the fire incinerated its prehistoric flesh and turned it to ash, what it was conveying became perfectly clear, and even though the giant *Chelydra Serpentina* has been dead for nearly twenty years, it only stopped talking to me recently.

It all began when I was tossing around a football with my best friend, Dennis, and some older kids emerged from behind the cluster of trees concealing a tiny stream in back of the elementary school we attended. They were carrying a large object to a barrel used by the school's janitor, Mr. Johnson, to burn trash. When they reached it, they lowered it into the rusty metal container, letting it drop the last couple of feet with a loud thud.

"What do you think they're doing?" I asked Dennis, who suggested we go see.

Another boy approached carrying a small tin can.

"Here's the kerosene," he announced and poured it into the barrel.

Dennis braved the question about what they were up to and was told they were going to set fire to a turtle.

"Why?" I inquired incredulously, and the boy with the fuel can answered that they were burning it as an experiment.

"We want to see what it does. See if its shell keeps it from melting. Besides, it's just a nasty old snapper. No good for nothing," he added, tossing the empty container to the ground a few feet from where we stood.

"Okay, here goes," announced another kid, striking a wooden match and dropping it into the barrel.

Flames leapt up instantly, and everyone took a few steps back in awe. In the whoosh of the flames I heard a squealing sound, but Dennis claimed he didn't. When the flames settled down after a few minutes, everyone closed in on the barrel except me.

"Come on, let's look," said Dennis excitedly.

"That's wrong!" I replied, but he ignored my protest and joined the boys peering into the barrel.

"You shouldn't do that," I shouted but no one paid attention to me.

Again, I heard a squeal emanate from the barrel, but this time it was followed by a series of sharp grunts that mixed with the crackling and snapping of the flames spewing embers into the air.

"It's suffering," I protested, and was told to shut up by the oldest of the boys, who was probing the depths of the barrel with a stick.

"It's still moving," he announced ecstatically, and everyone, including Dennis, eagerly took a turn poking at the baking creature.

"I'm going to tell," I warned, and the big kid, who obviously was the leader of the group, said if I did I'd be sorry.

"Well, I am getting the police," I threatened, and he waved his clenched fist at me menacingly.

That was when the turtle first spoke to me.

"They know not what they do, so leave them to their senseless deed," it said.

More than a little startled I probed the expressions of the other boys to see if they, too, had heard the words of the dying reptile. It was clear they had not, because they continued to behave with gleeful abandon as they stared into the barrel.

"I think it's dead," claimed one of the boys.

"No, it's still moving," responded another.

"It's roasted," observed yet another. "No way it can be alive."

But it *was* alive, because it kept speaking.

"Nothing ever really perishes," it declared, adding, "Things become something else, but they continue to exist. So don't fret, young man. You are good to care for me and see the wrong in what they do, but there is nothing more you can do. You have done what any decent and noble living thing should. You have opposed cruelty, and I commend you for doing so."

Still, I wanted to beat up the boys for killing the turtle, and I was mad at Dennis for going along with them and not joining me in trying to prevent their malicious act.

After about a half-hour, the oldest boy pronounced the turtle officially dead and the others, including Dennis, agreed, each carefully examining the barrel's depths. By that time, I had retreated to the edge of the field, and when Dennis waved at me, I turned to run for home.

"It's dead! It's dead!" they sang out and began marching around the smoldering tomb as if engaged in some primitive ritual.

I told no one about the turtle talking to me that day, and although it has spoken to me ever since, I have not dared to reveal this, fearing I would be thought crazy, even by those closest to me.

"Kids can be so cruel," commented my mother when I told my parents what happened.

"Well, it was only a turtle," replied my father, folding the day's newspaper in half and placing it on the coffee table.

"Still, that's not a very kind thing to do," said my mother shaking her head in disapproval.

"People make soup of those things, you know," added my father. "It's not like they're human."

"But burning it to death. That's just wrong," I chimed in.

"It *is* wrong," agreed my mother. "The poor thing. It deserved better."

"You two are just like each other," snapped my father, and I nodded in happy agreement as he lifted the paper from the coffee table and began reading it again.

After the grim episode of that day, I stopped hanging out with Dennis, and a year later my family moved to another part of town. A decade passed before I saw him again. We bumped into each other in a bookstore. We were both attending college, and he was there looking for a title he needed in a course, and I was there scanning the mythology section, a subject that came to interest me greatly.

Despite my continuing dialogue with the turtle, he remained very secretive about himself, so I began to study up on turtles and the myths that different cultures ascribe to them. The one I liked best claimed that turtles possessed the wisdom of the world. That was certainly true of the one that had befriended me and imbued my thoughts with its sage insights and perspectives on the meaning and purpose of existence.

At first my conversation with Dennis was a bit awkward, but then we both seemed to relax a little over a cup of coffee. He was majoring in business and already was engaged to someone he had dated throughout high school. He was impressed when I told him I was in pre-med with plans to attend veterinary school.

"You always were kind of a brain," he replied, "and a little weird, too, but in a good way," he added with a slight chuckle.

It took some gumption for me to ask if he remembered the burning turtle incident, but it was something I felt compelled to do. I had never reconciled how my best friend could go along with such a heinous act.

"What? Say that again," he replied in a perplexed tone.

"You know, when those older boys put a turtle in a barrel and burned it to death," I pressed.

"Man, I don't remember that at all," he answered looking like he'd just caught a whiff of something rancid.

"Come on," I protested, "you couldn't have forgotten that."

"Well, if it happened, I sure don't remember it. Kids do a lot of weird things. You can't remember all of them. What's the big deal anyway? It was just a turtle. Not like someone was killed."

I could feel the blood rush into my cheeks and my body tense up. How could he forget such a horrible thing? Was he just pretending not to recall what was one of the most disturbing and altering experiences of my life? It was then that I lost it.

"You creep! It was a helpless creature you helped kill, and it was so much more than that…more than you could ever know!"

With those words I stormed out of the bookstore's café before I gave in to the urge to clobber him. In the years since, thanks to the wisdom of the burning turtle, I have come to better understand people like Dennis and those who act with such utter disregard for life. From it I also learned forgiveness. It was the hardest lesson of all but the one that rewarded me most.

"Let go resentment for it sours the soul and blocks the path to true fulfillment," it advised, and I did.

The turtle had enhanced every aspect of my life and I felt blessed that it had chosen to guide me through the challenges and travails confronting me as I made my way through the years. My relations with all living things transcended the commonplace because of its devoted tutelage.

It was not long after my son entered the world that the voice of the turtle went silent, and I knew with complete certainty that it had migrated into my newborn. No parent could have been happier or wish for anything more for their child. At his christening the minister chose to read a verse from the bible that meant more to me than he could ever imagine.

> *Rise up my love, my fair one, and come away*
> *For lo, the winter is past, the rain is over and gone;*
> *The flowers appear on the earth; the time of the*
> *singing of birds is come, and the voice of the turtle is*
> *heard in our land.*

How to Kill Yourself

He still loves life,
but O O O O how he wishes
the good Lord would take him.
— W.H. Auden

Over the years Martin and Ann Purdue discussed the idea of doing themselves in when they got too old or infirm to care for themselves or maintain basic physical proficiencies—like bladder and bowel control. Childless, the last thing they wanted was to become housebound or a burden to their few remaining relatives because of declining health. The thought of getting old weighed heavily on them and now in their early 70s they realized they needed a plan to avert the despair and humiliation that inevitably lay ahead. Departing together made sense because neither of them could imagine life without the other. They had seen what losing a spouse did to friends, and that definitely was not the road they wished to travel.

"Who wants to live like that?" observed Ann as they lingered in bed after an uninspired sexual interlude, talking about the pitfalls of aging.

"Not me," replied Martin, sitting up and searching for his underwear among the tangled bed sheets.

"The whole getting old thing is such a bad design. Nature sure could have done better," declared Ann, staring at the leafless winter tree beyond the bedroom window.

"It stinks," added her husband, tugging his shorts over his spindly hairless legs. "Why bother? You've outlived your value to the world anyway. Nobody is interested in what old people think or have to say. Not really. They pay you lip service but sure as hell don't want to hang out with you."

"I don't want to live like that," said Ann, looking at the liver spots on the backs of her hands.

"Maybe it's time," suggested Martin. "I can start looking for ways to do it. Should have started looking long ago."

"Okay," replied Ann, rising from the bed and wincing from the ever-present pain in her lower back. "But I don't want us to suffer. No messy exits. I just want to go gently with you."

"Go to sleep with each other and just not wake up," said Martin rubbing the problem area of his wife's back.

After breakfast, he fired up his seven-year-old Epson PC and searched "How to kill yourself." He was impressed by the number of hits he got and surprised at the humorous and satirical nature of many. While the subject was no laughing matter to him, he could not help but be somewhat amused when one site featured the theme song "Suicide Is Painless" from the TV show *M*A*S*H*. He fervently hoped it would be.

Another site blithely suggested half a dozen methods for ending one's existence:

Blow yourself up with a homemade bomb.

Drown in your own urine while standing on your head.

Gather enough fur from your cat to choke on a hairball.

Play dodge ball with a live grenade.

Use anthrax to sweeten your coffee.

Clean the toilet bowl of a hospital restroom with your tongue.

Yet another recommended over 100 ways to kill yourself. Those that tickled Martin's funny bone the most had recommended eating a tubful of beans, head butting the sidewalk, watching the Lifetime Channel for one week, angering a cannibal, swallowing vanilla bath beads, accompanying a friend on a flight in his homemade plane, and using Draino to prep for a colonoscopy.

Clearly there were a lot of people having fun at the expense of those seriously searching for ways to end their life sans unpleasantness, thought Martin, as he continued to scroll down the results of his search. To his relief, not all of the sites made a joke of the subject, but most of those earnest about assisting the suicide candidate first advised counseling.

"Many people often feel that life is not worth living, but on reexamination find that it is," was their common message.

Martin discovered that many sites purporting to provide information about terminating life were more intent on directing people to various religions and deities. One site flashed 1-800-SEEKGOD accompanied by a figure of a hangman's noose intersected by a large red X. *About as subtle as a Mack truck*, he thought. Despite this, Martin stuck with it and went pages deep into his search results, finally coming upon what he felt would be the best approach to his question. "Take a hundred pills of any prescription-strength barbiturate with a glass of water and you will enjoy everlasting sleep." *So it's as easy and simple as that*, Martin reflected, quitting his computer.

Acting on this advice he and wife decided to stockpile pills for the inevitable moment when they reached the end of their tolerance for the debilitations of old age. It would require they make visits to their individual doctors claiming the need for sedatives until they accumulated all that was necessary to do the job. Doing exactly that, they soon had in excess of 200 bromides prescribed for the acute anxiety attacks they both claimed to be suffering.

"Well, these should do the trick when we're ready," observed Martin confidently.

They stored the pharmaceuticals in their separate medicine cabinets for use when they chose to implement their plan, and knowing they had a way to end their compromised existences provided them renewed gusto for the time that remained.

Over the next two years, they traveled extensively and enjoyed relatively good health, but then the boom dropped when each was diagnosed with chronic conditions that substantially restricted their activities. Ann's cardiovascular disease was more serious than her husband's rheumatism, which he was able to mitigate with acupuncture and physical therapy.

Nonetheless, they concluded the time had arrived to execute their plan and they set a date. They had not wavered in their resolve to stem the grotesque mutation of their bodies. The plan was to attempt to enjoy the holidays with their cousins and on New Year's Eve overdose and end the travesty that was late life. When the moment was upon them to act, they did.

Martin emptied the three vials containing his pills onto his bedroom nightstand and Ann did likewise with hers. Next he turned on the CD player containing their favorite piece by Debussy, one they had made passionate love to in better days. Ann removed the cork from a bottle of Moet and filled their glasses. Alcohol could only heighten the effect of the pills, they figured, and why not a champagne toast to commemorate such a momentous occasion? They had lived their lives as best they could, remaining happily married for the better part of a half-century, and they believed that was certainly worth celebrating.

"To you, my dearest," said Martin raising his glass.

"Back at you, sweetie," Ann replied, and they clinked glasses.

"Shall we?" he asked, pointing to their individual piles of pills.

"It's as good a time as any," his wife replied, and they both swallowed several mouthfuls of their medications along with many glasses of the bubbly.

They then settled back on the bed and wrapped their arms around one another, proclaiming their eternal love until a deep sleep overtook them and death followed…that is, for Ann. Martin awakened many hours later in a profound fog, his wife's motionless body next to him. When his head cleared he searched for her pulse, but there was none. She was dead and he was not. *How could that possibly be?* he wondered, his mind swirling and heart sinking.

The better part of an hour passed before Martin could bring himself to leave his wife's side. By then he had decided to dispose of any evidence of their suicide pact before contacting the authorities, hoping they would view her death as natural. He removed the prescription containers but left the empty champagne bottle on his night table. He would tell the police they had toasted the New Year before turning in for the night. He hoped his wife's consumption of alcohol would be viewed as a possible contributing factor in her death thus allaying suspicion of an overdose.

And so it was. Ann's body was removed from the house by ambulance attendants, who seemed to regard her passing as just another old person checking out. The accompanying police behaved similarly, expressing their condolences to Martin who was appropriately and genuinely grief-stricken. Three days later Ann Purdue was buried and Martin was left to contemplate the desolation of life without her. Why she had died when he had not plagued him, and he determined to ascertain the reason for such a cruel twist of fate. He began his investigation with his longtime doctor to check on the medicine he had been prescribed. Lately he had started to suspect it was not what it was purported to be, and his inquiry ended when his physician admitted that he had given Martin placebos rather than the real thing.

"You're one of the most stable people I know, so I figured they'd do the trick. Sorry they haven't," he explained, and Martin had his answer.

He did not confront his doctor on the issue because he felt it would just raise questions about his wife's passing. In fact, he even accepted his doctor's offer for actual sedatives figuring he could still give suicide-by-tranquilizers another shot, although he now doubted the efficacy of this method. While it had worked on his wife he remembered she had been diagnosed with a weak heart and very low blood pressure, which he figured may have enhanced the drug's potency. He would need to do something more definitive, he concluded, and returned to the Internet for a better solution. Despite all his searching, the most common techniques—hanging, jumping, and shooting—remained the most popular and reliable ways to "off" yourself, as one site called it.

After a couple weeks of reflection, he decided that shooting himself in the head was the surest way to guarantee the result he sought. For his 21st birthday Martin had received a gift that would assist in his new suicide plan. It was his father's prized souvenir from his WWII days—a German Lugar. Only occasionally would the elder Purdue display it and then he would do so with much ceremony and the inevitable account of how it came into his possession. Martin had been intrigued by it from the first time he laid eyes on it as a young boy, and so it was quite an auspicious occasion when his father turned it over to him for safekeeping. Although he had never fired it, Martin had kept it fully loaded in his nightstand in case of intruders. It gave him a feeling of security in these troubled times, although it made his wife nervous to have a gun in the house.

"A criminal could turn it on us," she would warn with a shudder of disapproval.

"He'd have to wrestle it from me first," responded Martin, and she would remark that knowing that did not make her feel any better.

"Get rid of it," she would plead, but he never did, and now he was grateful for that as he took the weapon from the drawer, put it to his head, and pulled the trigger.

But nothing happened. Martin pressed the trigger again, but the result was the same. In frustration and anger he tossed the pistol across the bedroom and began to weep. As the minutes passed he began to focus on the absurdity of his failed suicide attempts.

"Shit," he cried out in the empty room and then curled up in a fetal position on the bed he and his dead wife had slept and made love in for most of their adult lives.

While he had not given up on the idea of killing himself, he decided he would try to assuage his despair by attending a grief counseling group meeting held at the local Methodist church. The members of the assemblage ranged in age from 50 to 80 and all had lost a loved one recently. Martin took some comfort in their stories but often found himself more depressed because of them.

It was at the third meeting that he struck up a conversation with a recent widow who sat next to him. In many ways she reminded him of Ann, although she was a good ten years younger. What he found most appealing about her was the warmth and sweetness she exuded, and despite the recent tragedy in her life, she would laugh in a way that lifted his spirits. They soon started seeing each other regularly, and before the year was out, they were married. Each day Martin's existence seemed to become less burdensome and more pleasurable. During their brief courtship Martin had Googled, "How to live life to its fullest," and a statement on a website became his mantra. It read: "Death is inevitable, so why waste time worrying about it?"

Later that same day, while cleaning out his medicine cabinet in advance of his move to a new house with his bride, he came across Ann's empty tranquilizer container that had held her suicide pills. There were two refills remaining on the prescription. Without hesitation, Martin tossed the vial into the trash basket. He then stood before the mirror and stared at his image for several minutes. Gradually, the smile on his face turned to a frown.

"Shit," he muttered, and fished the pill bottle out of the trash.

Smoke Dreams

And my childish wave of pity
— John Betjeman

When I was ten years old, I started a fire at a hotel. That was back in 1958, and it was at one of the many fleabags my father and I occupied during the years I bummed around the country with him. On that particular occasion he was sleeping off another in an endless series of drunks while I restlessly awaited his return to consciousness by losing myself in my active fantasy world. It was a refuge from the bleak moments with an alcoholic parent who had been on a downward spiral most of his adult life. During my infrequent stays with my mother and two younger sisters, my mother would attempt to enlighten me about his checkered past in the hope it would break the firm hold he had on me.

"I know you care for him, but he's just so irresponsible, and his drinking ruins everything. Look what he's done to this family. Why do you think I divorced him? I don't understand the strong attraction he has for you. You're drawn to him like a moth to a flame," she would lament at every possible opportunity.

Despite her common sense pleadings, the allure of the freewheeling gypsy's life with my father would inevitably win out. With him I would not have to endure the tedium and routine of school, church, and weekly baths, none of which held great appeal for me. With him every day was an adventure, which despite the toll it would eventually exact from me, was what I wanted. I could not get enough of the open road. The hum and swoosh of the passing cars, as we stood with our thumbs outstretched, was the irresistible siren call that beckoned me, so I would take off with him. Just like that, I'd be gone. Vanished from the care of my mother. On the way to school or after school, I would meet up with my old man (after all he was over 50), and we would slip away undetected, leaving my mother to agonize over my whereabouts and well being.

"You don't know how it would tear at my heart," she would tell me years later when I was old enough to better appreciate her pain.

She would not call in the police to investigate my disappearance. She knew I was with my father and she knew it was my choice to go with him. That fact had long been established. Besides she had my two younger sisters to care for and did not need the added upheaval an investigation might cause, reasoning that it would jeopardize the tenuous domestic stability she had worked so hard to create.

* * *

The most recent round of wandering the country with my father had run its course, and I was interested in spending another hiatus, a breather from the road, with my mother and sisters. We had no real plan or destination at that moment, having just returned from the West Coast two weeks earlier. As had been the case with our previous odysseys to places we imbued with grandiose significance, things had not turned out the way we imagined they would. Alas, I had not been discovered for a role in the movies, something I felt was my destiny, and my father's hope of securing a bellhop job at the famous Beverly Hills Hotel had been dashed when he was informed that there had not been an opening there in years.

"They hold onto to those gigs because they make big tips from the famous actors who come to town," was his gloomy assessment.

So things had reached another low ebb, and I was really down in the dumps—as low as an ant's underpants, to quote my father. As I paced the drab room in the crumbling hotel in downtown Providence, Rhode Island, all I could think about was the hole in my life caused by the recent loss of my toy guns and rhinestone studded holster. Later when reunited with my mother she would accuse my father of pawning them. He would claim he had done no such thing, his thick eyebrow arching nearly to his thinning widow's peak. He looked like the actor Robert Taylor when he did that, and he knew it.

"What the hell would they give me for a toy anyway, for chrissakes? They don't buy that crap!"

He is wrongly accused and exhibits appropriate indignation, flicking the remains of his cigarette into the air causing a contrail of orange sparks. But the truth is my cherished pistol and holster set, which I have had since my last birthday, is lost. Not hocked, as my father makes dramatically clear, but gone just the same.

My wild west six-shooters, with plastic pearl handles and gem encrusted holster, were being withheld due to an unpaid locker fee at the Providence train depot. A dime is good for twenty-four hours.

How I longed for my authentic Colt replicas. How I mourned their absence. They were my prized possessions. When they hung from my narrow hips, I was everything I dreamed of being. Hopalong Cassidy astride Topper. Tall and invincible.

Shortly after we arrived back in Providence—the city we spent most of our time hating and escaping and inevitably returning to because it was our home base of sorts, due to its proximity to my mother and sisters—my father began boozing and we were booted from the dingy rooming house that had let us stay there without paying the customary rent in advance. My father decided we should not cart around our stuff, which was squeezed into a dilapidated brown canvas suitcase with hard cowhide handles, so he stored them in a railroad station locker. Our worldly belongings, including my shiny revolvers, were pushed into the dark boxy abyss.

"We'll pick them up when we get another place to stay," assured my father, patting the top of my head.

"You can't walk around with those on, Mikey, even if they are fake," he explained, adding that we had to make a good impression if we expected anybody to extend us credit until he got a job.

He winked at me in complicity. I was his little partner, he said in a secretive voice, a smirk on his unshaven face. It made me feel good when he said that. Sometimes not so good, especially when I thought of my mother enumerating his legion defects.

"He's a drunkard! A sad example of a human being. Burns everything he touches," she begins each vitriolic rant.

Days later when he was sleeping off the effects of a tankard of cheap wine, I knelt next to our bed in yet another roach infested rooming house and observed a spasm in his woolly chin and lower lip and a drop of murky liquid form and creep from the corner of his clenched and quivering right eye to the bridge of his ample nose. He mumbled something that sounded like, "Please...please don't. I will...honest" while I removed the locker key from his pants pocket. That accomplished, I ran like a gazelle through the bustling intersection's of Providence's congested center, past the Outlet and Shepherd's department stores, where my father claimed he had tried to get sales jobs, to the train station at the summit of a small bedraggled downtown park mostly occupied by other drunks and lost souls.

My heart pounded not from physical exertion—I could run for miles without the slightest sign of fatigue—but from the anticipation of a reunion with something very dear. When I caught sight of the brick edifice of the depot, I accelerated my pace and narrowly escaped the fender of a delivery truck. In the glass of the station's large swinging doors, I could see the truck stopped in the middle of the street and the driver shaking his fist at my back.

A few feet away from the wall of gray lockers, I applied the breaks and slid across the slick marble floor to number 16, the vault containing my treasure and joy.

As I dug into my pocket for the key, I noticed a black seal covering the lock. I pulled at it, but it did not budge. Next I looked around to make certain there was no other locker numbered 16. There was not, and I began to panic. How could that be? Had my pistols been stolen? I speculated as my sense of dread deepened.

When I explained my predicament to a matchstick thin and leathery skinned black man in a red cap and dark uniform, reminiscent of the ones worn by theater ushers, he observed that when the time runs out on the lockers, the contents are removed and held for additional payment. With a nonchalance that stood in dramatic counterpoint to my mounting hysteria, he added that every day it costs more to get stuff back.

"If ya ain't got no dough, sonny, ya cain't get da goods," he explained, with a slack-jawed smile that revealed two brilliant gold caps separated by a discolored front tooth.

Stunned by this information and unwilling to accept the terrible implication of it, I tried opening several adjacent lockers, although their numbers did not match those on my key. To compound my frustration, the key fit into every lock but then could not be turned. So close but yet so far, my father would say.

I wanted to rip the door off of every locker, which had now become tiny impenetrable crypts to me. Make a scene. Fall to me knees and cry…scream. Maybe that would have inspired the sympathetic attention of the person holding my guns for ransom. I ran a brief scenario in my head to ease my anguish. But I remained unarmed and unconsoled and left the station utterly defeated. As I wandered back to the seedy rooming house, I dragged the tops of my shoes against the pavement until the scuff marks appeared on the verge of becoming holes.

My father said not to worry. That he would get our things, and my toys, as soon as he got something to do to pick up a few bucks. I don't like the way he referred so dismissively to my priceless treasures. They are so much more than toys to me.

As the days passed it became painfully obvious to me that I would never see my gun set again. It would cost a bundle to get the stuff out, observed my father, who concluded it would be easier to just replace everything. Actually cheaper in the long run, he surmised.

"Your old lady couldn't have paid much for those dumb toys anyway. She got them at a yard sale," he revealed, and that surprised me because they were so neatly boxed and wrapped on my birthday.

After I visited the train station several more times in the hope that my guns and holster would magically reappear, I dropped the locker key through the grate of a sidewalk ventilation shaft on my way back to our present shelter.

When my father returned after a day of washing dishes and busing tables at a nearby diner—or "hash house" as he smugly called it— I shot him repeatedly with my index finger and thumb.

* * *

When he got his first paycheck we snuck out of the rooming house to avoid paying the back rent we owed. My father felt like a mogul with the two ten dollar bills in his pocket, and I knew a drink was on his mind. He deposited me at the Strand Theater, where a double feature was playing that I had been bugging him to see. He had no interest in cowboy pictures, he remarked as he coughed up the 35 cents it cost to get me in.

"Had enough of that western crap for a while," he remarked clearly alluding to our long and arduous journey across the rugged and desolate landscape of the southwestern desert, where we almost succumbed to the blazing sun after standing for days on Route 66 trying to hitch a ride.

"You go enjoy them, Mikey. I'll pick you up after the flicks."

"Don't drink," I beseeched him, as I entered the air-conditioned movie house.

When I emerged three hours later he was nowhere to be found. A half an hour passed before I spotted him approaching from a block away. He was weaving from the obvious affects of alcohol and my heart sank.

"How you doin', sonny boy," he slurred, and I cursed him. "Hey, watch your mouth," he snapped grabbing my hand and tugging me away from the theater entrance.

He dragged me to a nearby gin joint (one of the many terms he had for bars) until he was so blotto he could hardly stand, but to our saving grace he had rented a room at a hotel after dropping me off at the show earlier. On occasion he would actually take steps to secure us housing before launching his binge and that had been one of those times. Back in our room he dozed while I considered my next move. My plan was to get to my mother's in Westerly, some thirty or forty miles away. These intentions I had made clear to my father, who still was not keen on the idea, even though I had been pitching it to him since our return east.

"Hold off for a few days until I get us back on our feet again. I don't want your mother seeing you this way. I got to buy you some new things to wear first. That shirt you got on is pretty ragged and those dungarees have seen better days."

Those were his words earlier in the day as we made our escape from the rooming house where, as so many times before, we owed back rent. He had promised to find us a better place to lay our heads while I took in the double feature. As he sprawled out on the bed in an alcoholic stupor my resentment for him peaked. He was the "drunken bum" my mother called him, and he would never be anything else. Sure, we had our fun on the road, but things always turned out badly because of his addiction, what my mother once called his dipsomania.

It was at that moment in the shadowy gloom of the hotel room that the idea of setting the place on fire came to me. Where it originated, I cannot say. I'm sure it had its roots in my frustration and sense of hopelessness. Maybe I saw it as a way to attract attention to my dilemma, or maybe it was the first impulse of a future arsonist. Who knew for sure? Whatever it was and wherever it came from it had an overpowering affect on me and within seconds I had taken my father's tattered Zippo lighter from his jacket that hung over a chair and slipped into the bathroom. There I sat on the commode flicking the lighter's metal top back and forth while surveying my surroundings for something to ignite. My first thought was to put the lighter's flame to the towel draped over the side of the sink, but then I caught sight of a better target—toilet paper. It would catch fire faster, I figured, as I reached for it, unraveled some, and tore it from its roll. I then dangled it from my outstretched hand as I moved the lighter to its end. Without hesitation or a second thought, I ignited it and flames instantly shot up the paper column toward my hand. As the fire illuminated the bathroom, I was suddenly accosted by the horrifying realization that I was about to perpetrate a heinous crime, one that might not only take my father's life and mine but very likely the lives of many other people, who had nothing to do with the sad trajectory of my existence.

The heat of the flames registered sharp and hot on my fingertips as I heaved the ball of fire into the tub and turned on the faucet. The inferno was doused as quickly as it had been kindled, filling the bathroom with swirling shafts of gray putrid smoke. I watched as the remnants of burned toilet paper became wet ash and slithered down the drain. My fingers tingled from the burns, and for several minutes I held them under the stream of cold water that had thankfully dispatched the evidence of my would-be crime. *That's what you get for trying to kill your ole dad*, I could hear my father saying in my imagination, and then I became overcome by guilt and remorse for the murders I nearly committed.

When my father awoke a few hours later, he had the dry heaves. Between his pathetic retching sounds, he managed what seemed like a heartfelt apology, and my affection for him was revived.

"Sorry, Mikey. We'll get you to your mother's for a while. That would be better for you right now. Hey, how would you like to go to Florida in a month or two? We've never been there. It's great. Lotsa' beaches and palm trees. I can get a job at a hotel down there. I'll get some dough together, and we'll go, okay? What do you think?"

"Sure," I replied, keeping my hands in my pockets to hide my scorched fingers, which had become blistered.

* * *

The next day, I was transferred to the care of my mother, and during the three months I spent with her and my sisters, my imagination burned with the prospect of hitting the road again with my father to places I would come to learn only existed in the realm of our misbegotten dreams.

The Everlasting Sorrow of Silence

Deep-hearted man, express
Grief for thy dead in silence like to death;
Most like a monument statue set
In everlasting watch and moveless woe,
Till itself crumble to the dust beneath.
Touch it: the marble eyelids are not wet—
If it could weep, it could arise and go.
—Elizabeth Barrett Browning

My mother came back to life after being dead for two years. At midnight there was a tapping on the door, and there she was, Margaret Patricia Moore, looking better than during her last days on life support. My body stiffened and my heart thumped. Terror pinched my capillaries and the ground began to pull out from under me. *People do rise from the dead,* I reminded myself in an attempt to keep from coming totally unglued.

"Who's at the door?" inquired my groggy wife as she approached from the dark recesses of the hallway, and when she caught sight of my mother she let out such a deafening shriek I could not repress one of my own.

"Calm down, you two. You'll wake your neighbors. Can I come in?" asked our improbable visitor, a bemused grin on her pale face. "I feel a little light-headed. I haven't had anything to eat in quite a while."

It took a few protracted moments to overcome my shock enough to respond to her request.

"Of course, Margaret," I said, my voice shaking as I put my arm around my trembling wife. "Come into the kitchen. Can you walk?"

"I got here, didn't I?" she replied, a faint echo attached to her voice, "but it wasn't easy. My legs aren't what they used to be. Pretty much skin and bones, as you can see."

She lifted the hem of her skirt, revealing legs that had long lost their form and most of their function. The network of varicose veins that had plagued both her calves and her spirit were even more prominent as they levitated from her desiccated limbs—bulbous purple aneurysms on a rampage. After some effort I managed to navigate her to the kitchen table where she sat catching her breath as we quickly emptied the contents of the refrigerator before her.

"Leftover meatloaf. I love your meatloaf, Celia, but you know that, don't you, dear? I'll just have a sandwich with a smidgen of mayo. Put the rest of this stuff back in the icebox before it spoils." My mother swept her hand across the table's bounty. "I'm not that hungry, honey."

"You love pickles. How about a nice dill?" I said, unscrewing the jar and placing a spear on the plate before her.

"Lord knows that's true, and these look particularly lovely," she replied taking a tentative bite. "Flavor's a bit off, but I haven't used my taste buds in over two years."

Celia busied herself stacking slices of meatloaf on bread all the while fixated on my mother's every move. A mix of disbelief and apprehension altered her usually sunny expression.

"Would you like me to warm your sandwich in the microwave?" she offered, holding it before her on a plate.

"No, honey. It just turns stuff to leather," answered Margaret reaching for the sandwich. "Never liked those darn contraptions. They do something funny to things."

"I'm going to call my sisters," I said, as Margaret took her first bite.

"No you're not!" blurted Margaret, pieces of her chewed sandwich cascading from her lips. "I'm here for you, *not* them."

"What do you mean? They'll want to see you. I have to call them. They'd never forgive me if I didn't."

"Look, if there's still time, I'll see them, but you know returnees can be back for a very short time, and I have important business with you."

"Some have been back for days, even longer," I protested. "A man in Turkey was back for two weeks."

"Maybe, but that was two hundred years ago, so I don't think you can rely on that account."

Since such records were kept, eleven people had reportedly returned from the dead. The last known "resurrection," as some in the religious community called it, was sixty-seven years ago in a small farming community in western Iowa. No one but the returnee's husband had witnessed the visit. On the whole, accounts of returnees were sketchy, and some argued that they were just hallucinations or apparitions inspired by the profound grief of those left behind.

"Margaret, please, I *have* to call Sarah and Mary. It wouldn't be right not to," I continued to plead.

"I'm *Mother*, not Margaret! You're my child, and children don't call their mothers by their first names."

"So that's it? You've returned because I call you by your first name?"

"That and the fact that you never once told me you loved me. At least not since you were five and went with your father."

"That's not true."

"Don't tell me!" snapped my mother, pushing her sandwich across the table. "It's something I've been very aware of...painfully aware of, in fact. Do you know how it affects a parent when their child behaves in such a way?"

"I never meant to hurt you. It just…well, felt funny."

"It felt *funny* to tell your mother you loved her? It felt *funny* to call me Mother? Your father turned you against me. All he did was lie to everyone, and I'm sure he said things about me that made you think I was awful."

For over a decade, I had roamed the country with my miscreant father, only occasionally spending time with my mother and sisters. The fact that she let me go with the person she constantly derided as irresponsible, even though I genuinely wanted to go with him, made me feel she had abandoned me—that she didn't love me enough to keep me, or fight to keep me. In the end, I felt she had given me away. It was then I decided never to address her as mother, an appropriate form of punishment, I believed. In my mind, she had failed to earn that precious designation, and my grievance had survived into deep adulthood like scar tissue. It had lodged in my soul and refused to be exorcized even as my mother and I grew closer over the years.

My father suffered the same fate, because I quickly concluded that if he really cared for me he would not be taking us from town to town like common drifters, causing me to miss school and form no lasting friendships. While I was attracted to the unstructured gypsy lifestyle—crisscrossing the country provided me endless delight— I knew deep down a responsible parent would not be subjecting his kid to such a peripatetic existence. So no more addressing *him* as dad or father either. These ancient and honored sobriquets I duly removed for unfulfilled and neglected services.

"Please eat your sandwich, Mar…" I said moving the plate back in front of my mother while catching myself before addressing her by her first name again.

"I think bad people don't come back, and that's why your father didn't," she countered.

"Jeez, only a handful have, so that leaves a lot of bad people," was my repost to what struck me as an utterly absurd and self-righteous statement.

Celia looked as if she might bolt from the room at any moment, and as Margaret took another tentative bite of her sandwich I shot my wife a look of reassurance in the hope of staving off an emotional eruption that clearly was building in her.

"He wasn't a monster. Just missing something that makes people live a normal life," I replied with an increasing edge to my voice. It was the same argument we'd had so many times when she was alive. Now here I was having it with her when she was dead.

"Please don't use that tone with me. You know darn well that *normal* was not a word in his vocabulary. He had no idea how to treat a wife and kids. I thought if your father took care of you like he promised after we were divorced, I would be able to manage with your sisters, but that was foolish thinking on my part. I knew he wasn't up to it. While you and he were away on your trips, the girls and me got by, and it wasn't easy. He never gave us any money, and my low-paying job hardly made ends meet. But we survived, because I was a responsible parent. I worked and kept food on the table and a roof over your sisters' heads. Your father hardly fed you. When you'd come back from the road, you always looked so thin, and while you were with us, I'd try to put some meat back on your bones, but then you'd take off with him again. What was his allure anyway?"

"I was a kid and it was an adventure with him. I didn't realize it wasn't the best thing for me. I just knew I didn't have to do all the things regular kids had to, like go to school and attend church."

"And take baths and wear clean clothes. You always looked dirty when you came back. I'd have to scrape the grime from your ankles. What kind of a life is that for a child? Your father had no concept of what was the right way to raise you. He just thought of himself and dragged you around with him. It was probably the alcohol, but *I* think he was born with something missing, too. A lot of drunks know what the right thing to do is, but not that man. Sober he was no better. Always discontent and looking for something else. Something besides the wife and three kids he had."

Again, she pushed the plate containing the remains of her sandwich across the table.

"Would you like some tea?" inquired Celia, her arms wrapped tightly around her chest as if to keep her from listing and falling over.

"What I'd like is some respect from your husband for being a mother who tried to do the right thing by him and his sisters. Even though he wasn't around most of the time, I never stopped thinking about him. It tore me up that he was away from us and with that man, who couldn't even care for himself let alone a child."

"I'm sure it was hard," responded Celia sympathetically.

"I know what you went through," I added, placing my hand on my mother's shoulder.

"So why do you continue to punish me?"

"I don't punish you," I responded defensively.

"You let me take my heartbreak to the grave, and that's cruel and unusual punishment, as far as I'm concerned."

Celia moved in the direction of the kitchen door and excused herself saying she was going to let us continue our conversation in private.

"Thank you, honey," replied Margaret, adding, "You've always been so considerate, unlike someone else we both know."

"I don't think that's fair. I did everything I could for you, and I think you know that, too," I protested as Celia made her exit.

"Well, not quite everything, but I'll admit that you were pretty decent to me in most things, and that helped some, but the pain of being denied what is due is pretty hard to live with…and *die* with."

"Denied?" I asked. "What do you mean?"

"Do I have to repeat myself? You stopped calling me 'Mother,' and only once or twice did you say you loved me, and that was after I put you on the spot by saying I loved you first. You were forced to say it out of a sense of obligation, because others were present. You didn't want them to think you were heartless. You did it to save face, not out of genuineness."

Tears began to well up in my mother's eyes, yet I felt as much irritation with her as sympathy. Throughout my life, it had seemed to me she had played the martyr card, casting herself as one of life's foremost victims. True, she'd had a difficult past. Orphaned by her alcoholic father whose wife had run away, leaving him with two young daughters he couldn't deal with, and then she herself was saddled with a reprobate for a husband. It was understandable that she would view herself as wronged, but in my opinion she exploited it, and for my benefit. It was not until I was in middle age and she in old age that I began to comprehend that she played the martyr out of a sense of guilt. I realized she, too, felt she had abandoned me and wanted me to understand and appreciate why and forgive her. Despite that I could not let go of my need to withhold the recognition she so acutely craved.

As I stood across from my mother in the awkward silence, she grew smaller and less physically palpable, a gossamer image. In that moment, and for the first time ever, I felt intense compassion and uninhibited affection for her.

"I love you, Mother!" I cried out, joining her chorus of sobs.

With the utterance of those words—words she had sought into eternity—she grasped my hand with her cold fingers and then gently withdrew them. An expression of measureless satisfaction transformed her fading countenance and, in the flicker of a moment, I was staring at an empty space where she had sat.

Wrapped in an Enigma

It is a riddle wrapped in a mystery inside an enigma.
— Winston Churchill

Among the things Mark Cowell most hated as a kid back in the primitive days of the mid-1950s was going to the store for what his mother cryptically called her "woman things"—as in "You've got to pickup my woman things." He had asked her what the mysterious brown box contained after being teased by some older boys on the way home from Zip's Variety.

"Ignore them," she advised, placing the anonymous carton on the top shelf of the bathroom closet. "They're just immature boys."

"What are Vlad Rags?" he asked repeating one of the terms they used for the package he was carrying.

"What? I never heard that one before," she replied with a smirk that further aroused his curiosity.

"They said you have the curse," he continued. "What does that mean?"

"They don't know what they're talking about," she said, her expression hardening. "Stay away from those kids. They sound really stupid. You're a whole lot smarter than they are."

Mark was nine and felt caught in a mystery he could not solve or understand. It took a handwritten note by his mother to obtain the product she wanted, and that added to his growing wariness about what he was transporting the three long blocks from Zip's to his house. The next time he was sent on the arcane errand, he asked Mr. Zipola if he would put the troublesome box in a bag to conceal it.

"Why you needa da bag? You only gotta' one ting and it easy to carry, lil' boy. You go take it to you mama. She need…she need now," he responded with a combination of irritation and urgency in his gruff voice.

What is the need he referred to? Mark wondered, his apprehension growing. As fate would have it on his return trip home he encountered the same menacing kids as before. While attempting without success to conceal the box under his arm, he increased his pace to get passed them.

"Hey, wait up. Let's see what you got?" said the biggest of the boys trailing close behind Mark.

"Yeah, give that to us," said his friend yanking the box from him.

"It's for my mother and she needs it!" he protested trying to grab it back.

Before Mark could do a thing—not that he could have, given their size and number—they tore the box open and fished out its contents.

"Hey, stop!" he shouted now convinced that whatever was in the box was crucial to his mother's continuing existence.

"Lookie here, snot head, you know what this is? It's a Kotex pad. Bet you never saw one of these before. Your mom's riding the bloody bronco," said the kid who'd snatched the carton from his hands.

His two friends laughed and removed other pads from the box while Mark stood there feeling helpless and embarrassed.

"Women use these so they don't bleed all over the place. What'd you think was in the box? Tootsie Rolls?"

"I know what they are," Mark objected. "Give them back to me, or I'll…"

"What? Tell the cops we stole your mommy's Kotex?"

"Yeah, bet they'd arrest us for that. Maybe give us the chair," joked another boy who until now had remained in the background.

"They're good if you got a big wound. They used them in the war to keep the soldiers from bleeding to death. Tape them on like a big ol' Bandaid," said the kid who towered over his friends. "Say you got a bullet right here," he continued placing the pad on his private area to the delight of everyone but Mark.

By now he was convinced his mother was in dire need of the healing power of the gauzy objects, and he began to have images of her lying in a pool of blood on the living room floor awaiting his arrival. Fearing for her well being, he suddenly found the courage to take a stand wrenching the pads from his tormenter's hands and dashing away before they knew what had happened. Amazingly he managed to reach his house before being caught, and he stormed through the front door shouting full throttle for his mother while expecting to encounter a gruesome scene.

"What?" she replied emerging from the kitchen looking fit as Esther Williams. "What the…what happened, for heaven's sake!" she blurted catching site of her son clutching the Kotex pads and gasping for air.

"Here," he said, handing her the few Kotex he had managed to seize. "You'll be okay, right? You won't die?"

"Die? Who told you that?" she asked completely perplexed. "Where's the box they were in? What's going on?"

His mother listened attentively while he gave her a complete account of his disturbing experience on the way home with her package of woman things, and when he finished she hugged him and gently kissed his forehead.

"What's wrong with you, Mom?" he asked still full of trepidation.

"There's nothing wrong with me, honey," she replied, reassuringly.

"Then why are you bleeding?" he asked and after a long pause she gave an answer that only compounded his confusion.

"Don't worry about it. It's not that bad, honey," she stammered adding, "You'll understand someday."

The next few times Mark went to Zip's for his mother—something he insisted on doing despite her concern—he managed to elude his antagonists, who eventually lost interest in him and his cargo. It was not until he was a couple years older that he learned women experience blood loss every month, and then his mother told him something that greatly lifted his spirits.

"I don't need them anymore," she told him wistfully.

"So how come you look sad, Mom?" asked Mark perplexed by her look of melancholy.

"Oh, nothing, honey," she replied with a sweet smile. "Just feeling old."

Mothers sometimes are very hard to understand, he thought, wondering why she would feel sad about finally being cured.

Breinigsville, PA USA
18 December 2010
251740BV00001B/8/P